It was the child's eyes that caused his heart to lurch.

Those were his eyes. And they were unmistakably the Wade family dimple that dipped into one side of Tucker's daughter's baby-soft cheeks.

His daughter. A barrage of emotions swept over Tucker as he stood looking down at her. He was a father. That revelation had his world tilting.

"Are you all right?" Autumn asked. "You look mighty pale."

He gave a forced laugh. "I'm better than all right. I'm a daddy."

"Tucker?" Autumn said, bringing him back to full awareness.

He blinked hard and then cleared his throat. "Sorry," he said. "This is a lot to take in."

"Would you like to call someone?" she suggested. "One of your brothers perhaps?"

The only time he'd ever come close to passing out had been when he'd gotten bucked off Little Cyclone during the Pioneer Days Rodeo up in Lander several years back. However, the little bombshell Autumn Myers had dropped on him just moments before had nearly managed to do what Little Cyclone hadn't been able to.

Bring this Montana-bred cowboy to his knees.

Nearly.

Kat Brookes is an award-winning author and past Romance Writers of America Golden Heart® Award finalist. She is married to her childhood sweetheart and has been blessed with two beautiful daughters. She loves writing stories that can both make you smile and touch your heart. Kat is represented by Michelle Grajkowski with 3 Seas Literary Agency. Read more about Kat and her upcoming releases at katbrookes.com. Email her at katbrookes@comcast.net. Facebook: Kat Brookes.

Books by Kat Brookes

Love Inspired

Bent Creek Blessings

The Cowboy's Little Girl

Texas Sweethearts

Her Texas Hero
His Holiday Matchmaker
Their Second Chance Love

The Cowboy's Little Girl

Kat Brookes

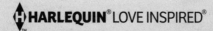

Recycling programs
for this product may
not exist in your area.

LOVE INSPIRED BOOKS

ISBN-13: 978-1-335-50963-5

The Cowboy's Little Girl

Copyright © 2018 by Kimberly Duffy

www.Harlequin.com

Printed in U.S.A.

Thanks be unto God for His unspeakable gift.
—*2 Corinthians* 9:15

I'd like to dedicate this book to
my wonderful agent, Michelle Grajkowski,
with 3 Seas Literary Agency. She has been
so incredibly supportive with my writing
endeavors, always believing in me. She's also
a dear friend. I feel so blessed to have her in
my life, both professionally and in friendship.

I would like to extend my deepest thanks to
Ryan Sankey from Sankey Pro Rodeo, who
offered me a wealth of information when I was
researching this rodeo-cowboy series. She
was always willing to answer any questions
I might have without hesitation. Sankey Pro
Rodeo has four Saddle Bronc of the Year PRCA
awards, twelve PRCA Stock Contractor of the
Year nominations, as well as many PRCA and
Montana Circuit awards. They've been featured
on ESPN, *USA TODAY*, *Western Horseman* and
CMT. More information on Sankey Pro Rodeo
can be found at www.sankeyprorodeo.com.

Chapter One

A persistent knocking at the front door of his ranch house had Tucker Wade setting the half-eaten grilled cheese he'd made himself for dinner back onto the plate beside him. Dropping his booted feet from the rough pine coffee table to the wood-planked floor, he stood to answer the door.

His first thought was that it was his oldest brother, Garrett, stopping by to shoot the breeze after returning from tending to Wilbur Davies's sick cow. Garrett, the town's only vet, had gotten called away, leaving Tucker and his other brother Jackson—older by just one year— to see to it the horses were fed and settled in for the evening. But his brothers rarely knocked. And if they did it was a loud, firm rap on the door, not the tentative tapping that had him moving into the front entryway. Not to mention it was near dark and they all followed an early-to-bed-and-early-to-rise routine.

Very little surprised Tucker, but nothing could have prepared him for the shock of opening the door to find his long-lost wife looking up at him. A woman he'd come to accept he would never see again. Didn't care to see again, truth be told. But there she stood, in the fiery red-orange light of the setting sun, looking every bit as pretty as he remembered and yet so very different.

The wispy blonde ponytail Summer had always worn had been replaced by a short, smooth haircut that hung longer in front than in the back. A formfitting navy skirt and matching jacket replaced her well-worn jeans and usual T-shirt. And… Tucker's gaze dropped lower, a dark brown brow lifting. *Heels?* The Summer he'd known would never have worn high heels, no matter how good they looked on her. Even her cowgirl boots had low heels. But then again, he'd only *thought* he'd known the girl he'd exchanged vows with six years before.

All the hurt, anger and confusion he had worked so hard to suppress after Summer took off without a word threatened to surface once again. Thickly lashed ice-blue eyes—eyes that had once held only warmth, now stared back at him with something akin to…mistrust? *Him.* The man *she'd* run out on.

"Tucker Wade?" his long-lost wife asked as if she wasn't quite sure it was him.

A frown tightened the line of his mouth. While he'd admittedly filled out a good bit in terms of muscle, no longer the lanky, bull-riding twenty-four-year-old she'd exchanged vows with at the Laramie County Courthouse, he was pretty certain she knew it was him. What sort of game was his wife playing now?

"I'm sorry to show up unannounced this way," she continued. "And this late in the day. But I had to meet with clients before setting out for Bent Creek."

There it was, that same Texas twang that had drawn him to his wife in the first place. "Why are you here?" he demanded.

Undaunted by the glower he was sending her way, she met his gaze head-on. "I thought it would be best if you heard what I have to say in person, instead of over the phone."

"*Now* you want to talk?" he said, anger writhing though him. "Well, this might come as a surprise to you, but I no longer have any interest in anything you have to say."

"I can't blame you for feeling the way you do," she said softly, "but if you'll just give me a chance to explain…"

"What are you doing here, Summer?" he cut in gruffly, not bothering to suppress the ire he felt toward her. He didn't want explanations. It was far too late for that. In fact, he wanted nothing at all from his wife.

"I'm not Summer." She looked away for a second as her voice filled with emotion. Then, looking up at him with those same silver-blue eyes he'd worked so hard to forget, she said, "I'm her sister Autumn."

What? Tucker blinked back his surprise. First, his wife shows up out of the blue, with no warning whatsoever of her impending arrival, and then she starts spouting nonsense? Who was Summer going to pretend to be next? A sister named Spring, or maybe Fall since it was mid-October? If his wife had a sister, he surely would have known about it.

Dear Lord, give me strength, he prayed.

"I know it's been a few years since we've crossed paths," Tucker grumbled in irritation, "but I'm pretty sure I haven't forgotten what my own wife looks like. Even with all that fancy polishing you've done to change your appearance." Which he begrudgingly had to admit looked really good on her.

She stiffened. "It's not polish. This is who I am."

He gave a derisive snort. "You forget who it is you're talking to. *This*," he said, waving a hand from her designer heels to her pretty little head, "is who you are until you decide the life you're living right now isn't really what you want. Then you'll just up and leave whoever it is who's fool enough to care about you at that time, without so much as a goodbye, and start a whole new life for yourself somewhere else." The jagged edge of the memory of what she'd done to him leaving the way she had all those years ago still cut deep.

She shifted uneasily. "She said you could be stubborn, but if you'll just hear me out…"

He had no idea why his wife had to be told by someone else, whoever "she" was, about his stubbornness. Especially when she used to tease him about it when they were dating. Or had she blocked everything about him and their marriage from her mind?

"I don't want your explanations," he said through tightly gritted teeth. It was five years too late for that. "Go back to wherever it is you came from, Summer. You don't have a place in my life anymore."

To his surprise, his clipped words brought a swell of tears to his wife's eyes. Her emotional response had him shifting uncomfortably where he stood. Maybe he had spoken a little harsher than he ought to have, but she'd done far worse to him all those years ago.

"I'm not Summer," she insisted once more. "And *she* won't be starting her life over," she added, her lower lip quivering slightly with that announcement. "At least not here on earth. My sister's gone."

Had his wife suffered a head injury of some sort? Was that why she was claiming to be someone else? "Sweetheart," he said, trying not to let the flood of emotions he felt at seeing her again show in his voice, "you're standing right here."

"Summer never told you about me, did she?" she asked as if she'd somehow been wronged. Then she shook her head and cast her gaze out across the yard. "No," she said sadly, "of course she didn't." Turning her attention back to him, she said, "I'm Autumn Myers. Summer's twin."

He raised a skeptical brow. "Her twin?"

She gave a slight nod. "Yes."

Tucker's gaze zeroed in on her slender perfectly arched brows, to where they disappeared just beneath the much shorter strands of hair that now framed his wife's heart-shaped face. "You have a scar," he heard himself saying.

"What?"

"The scar above your brow," he prompted with impatience.

"No," she said, "I don't." Reaching up, she pushed the hair away from her face.

"Other side," he muttered with a deepening frown. What kind of fool did she take him for? He'd been there when she'd gotten stitched up after her fall during one of her barrel races.

Without another word, she showed him her other brow. Even in the fading light of day, there was no denying the smooth expanse of skin where the scar had been.

Tucker struggled to drag in even the slightest of breaths. This woman standing before him was not his long-lost wife, no matter how much she resembled her. "Summer's dead?" he said, the words soft and gritty as he tried to process that something like that could even be true. She was so young. And while he had harbored a ton of resentment toward his wife after she'd walked away from the life they'd started together, to the point where he never ever wanted to see her again, this was not the way he'd wanted that to happen. Tucker's heart squeezed.

"Yes," Summer's twin replied. Never had one word been so filled with emotion.

"What happened?" he rasped out, finally accepting the truth for what it was. The woman that he'd once fancied himself in love with was dead. May she rest in peace.

"Summer took her horse out for a ride near our home in Cheyenne," she began, tears shimmering in her eyes.

"Summer was living in Cheyenne?" he muttered in disbelief. That was where his wife had chosen to put down roots? Not back home in Texas, in whatever town it was she had grown up in, but in Cheyenne. In the very place they had exchanged their wedding vows. How had they never crossed paths? Not that he'd stuck around very long once things ended.

"Yes," she began, the words catching as she looked up at him. "And if I had known about you…" She paused, shaking her head. "I'm afraid my sister didn't always think things out the way she ought to."

That was the Summer he remembered. But then that was another thing that had drawn him to her back then. They'd met at a rodeo, him a tough-as-grit bareback rider and her, a highly competitive barrel racer. They'd been young and reckless, looking to grab life by the horns and then hold on for wherever the ride might take them.

"I'm sorry," he said. "I didn't mean to interrupt. Knowing she'd lived so close just took me by surprise."

She nodded in understanding. "Summer was on her way back to the house when a rattlesnake spooked her horse and she was thrown." A sob caught in her throat with the last of her explanation.

"You don't have to say anything more," he told her, regretting the pain his question had caused her. While he no longer felt what he once had for his wife, Autumn Myers was still dealing with the grief brought about by the loss of her sister. He couldn't even begin to imagine how he would feel if he lost one of his brothers.

"It's all right," she assured him as she swiped a hand over her tear-dampened cheek. "As her husband, you have a right to know. My sister ruptured her spleen when she fell. They did emergency surgery to repair it, and she managed to hold on for a couple of days, but then infection set in and her body began shutting down."

Tucker closed his eyes, saying a quick prayer for the woman he'd married.

"That's when Summer opened up about the secrets she'd been keeping. *You* being one of them," she told him with a sorrowful frown. "I forgave her. I only pray the Lord did, as well."

Tucker dragged a splayed hand back through his thick chestnut hair, trying to digest everything she was telling him. It was hard to believe that the high-spirited, headstrong girl he'd once loved was gone.

"I'm sorry," he managed, the words coming out strained. He stood there, a part of him longing to close the door and shut reality out, pretend this moment had never happened.

"No," she mumbled despondently as her gaze shifted to the car she'd driven up in, which was parked a short distance from his house, "I'm sorry. You deserved to know the whole truth a long time ago. I pray that someday you'll be able to forgive my sister for the choices she made, as well."

"The whole truth?"

"There is something my sister should have told you about before walking away from your marriage," she answered.

"I'm not so sure it matters anymore," he told her. He was over any feelings he once had for his wife. There was nothing Autumn Myers could say to him that would change anything.

"You still should have the right to decide if it does one way or another," she said, her face a mask of determination.

It was clear she wasn't about to let things go, not until he'd heard her out. Tucker nodded. "If it will take some of the burden off your heart, then I'm willing to hear you out. Would you like to come inside and talk? I could fix you a glass of ice water or lemonade."

She nodded, her gaze drifting back toward her car once more. "But there's something I need to do first." With that, she turned and walked away.

Tucker stepped out onto the porch as he watched Autumn make her way to her car. It was clear her sister's death still weighed heavily on her, driving all the way across the bottom of Wyoming from Cheyenne to Bent Creek just to inform him in person of Summer's passing. Oddly enough, he found himself wishing he could say something that might set her mind at ease about what her sister had done. Something to let her know that it wasn't her burden to bear.

Her sister's passing. Nausea stirred in Tucker's gut at the very thought of it. Time and distance from the situation had made him realize how hastily he and Summer had gone into their marriage. They'd been too young and far too impulsive to place the proper amount of thought into what they were doing as they stood before the judge at the Laramie County Courthouse that day. And, yes, he'd been hurt, and more than a little confused, when she'd taken off the way she had. Anger had followed. It had taken a fair amount of praying and suffering months of inner turmoil trying to pinpoint exactly what it was that he'd done wrong to send Summer running before he'd finally come to accept that she'd made the right decision in ending their hasty marriage. Whatever her reason may have been.

Not that it had ended completely. Legally, they were still husband and wife, something he'd made no attempt to rectify. One failed marriage was enough for him. As long as he and Summer were still legally wed, he could never make the same mistake again. Giving his heart away to a woman and risking the possibility of it being trampled all over again was something he was determined to avoid at all cost. *Only now Summer is gone*, he thought with a pang of sorrow. And that made him a widower.

His attention shifted back to Autumn Myers's retreating form, noting with some confusion that instead of settling herself behind the wheel of her bright yellow Mustang GT she circled around to the rear passenger side. A soft, somewhat sad smile moved across her face as she reached out to open the back door.

He lost sight of her for a moment as she leaned into the back of the brightly colored sports car. A second later, she took a step back from the vehicle and motioned to someone in the back seat. A tiny head with a mass of long curls hopped out to join her.

With the little girl's hand tucked securely in her own, a now unsmiling Autumn held his gaze as she walked back to the porch. *She has a daughter*, he thought to himself. One she must have brought along to meet her uncle by marriage.

The fading rays of the afternoon sun glinted off the mass of curls that hung over the child's downturned face as they crossed the yard. Chestnut curls. An unsettling sensation moved through him. Why that was, he had no idea. He looked questioningly to Autumn as she guided her young daughter up onto the porch.

"Tucker Wade," she said before looking down at the little girl who now had her tiny face pressed into her mother's skirt, "this is my niece, Blue Belle Wade. That's Bell with an *e*," she clarified.

Tucker's thoughts scrambled to process the words she'd just spoken. *Her niece.*

"Blue," she continued, "this is—"

"My daddy?" the little girl mumbled as she dared an inquisitive peek up at him through the protective barricade of her reddish-brown curls that served to hide most of her face.

"Her what?" he gasped as her name filtered through his mind. Blue Belle. Summer's favorite flower. The same ones he'd given her a bouquet of when he'd asked her to marry him.

"Yes, sweetie," she answered, her tone tender. "This is your daddy." Autumn's gaze lifted to meet his. "Tucker Wade, meet your daughter."

His daughter. How was that possible? But her hair was the same reddish-brown shade as his own.

"Blue," Autumn said, gently nudging her niece, "say hello to your daddy."

His daughter's little face turned slightly as she peeked up at him. "Hello," she said timidly, burying her face once again in the soft fabric of her aunt's skirt.

Autumn ran a soothing hand down over her niece's curls. "Sweetie, we came all this way to meet your daddy. I think he deserves a chance to see that pretty smile of yours."

His little girl pulled away ever so slightly and tipped her chin upward. And then she smiled. The long spiraling strands of her hair fell away to reveal a heart-shaped face very similar to Summer's and Autumn's. But it was Blue's wide green eyes and the lone dimple that appeared when she smiled that caused his heart to lurch. Those were *his* eyes. And that was undeniably the Wade family dimple that dipped into one side of his daughter's baby-soft cheeks.

His daughter. A barrage of emotions swept over Tucker as he stood looking down at her. He was a father. That revelation had his world tilting. He struggled to steady himself as spots danced around in his vision.

"Tucker?" he heard Autumn say, concern lacing her voice. "Are you all right? You look mighty pale."

He gave a forced laughed. "I'm better than all right. I'm a daddy." Yet, even as he spoke his words of reassurance, darkness began to fringe his vision.

"How's come he's swaying like a tree in the wind?" he heard his daughter ask.

"Tucker?" Autumn said, the concern-filled utterance bringing him back to full awareness.

He blinked hard and then cleared his throat. "Sorry," he said. "This is a lot to take in."

"Would you like to call someone?" she suggested,

looking as if she expected him to drop into a dead faint any minute. "One of your brothers perhaps?"

The only time he'd ever come close to passing out had been when he'd gotten bucked off Little Cyclone during the Pioneer Days Rodeo up in Lander several years back. Landing on your head in a rodeo was cause for a little head spinning, yet he hadn't gone down. He was made of sturdier stock than that. However, the little bombshell Autumn Myers had dropped on him just moments before had nearly managed to do what Little Cyclone hadn't been able to—bring this Montana-bred cowboy to his knees. *Nearly.*

Tucker shook his head. "No need."

"You're really tall," Blue announced, craning her neck as she stood peering up at him.

He chuckled at Blue's observation, thankful that some of her shyness seemed to be easing up around him. "Not as tall as my brothers. Your uncles," he clarified. "They both top six foot. I'm only five foot eleven.

"I have uncles?" his daughter said excitedly.

It was hard not to let the injustice of what his wife had done, shutting him out of their child's life, seep into his tone. Summer had denied his parents the chance to get to know their only grandchild, and his brothers the opportunity to spoil their niece. "Two of them," he said with surprising calm, as the anger he'd once felt toward Summer after she'd walked out on their marriage returned to simmer just below the surface of his lighthearted demeanor.

"Do they live here, too?" asked Blue, looking around.

"No," he said. "This is my place. Your uncles have homes of their own that they live in on the ranch."

His daughter looked out over the land surrounding them. "I don't see them."

"That's because they're spread out across our family's nine-thousand-plus-acre ranch."

"What's an acre?"

"It's a measurement of land," Autumn explained.

"Do we have acres?"

"We do," she answered, glancing around. "But your daddy's property is a whole lot bigger than ours back in Cheyenne. We only have forty acres there and far fewer trees."

Blue swung her curious gaze back in his direction. "Do you have a swing set behind your house?"

"I'm afraid not," he said. "Never had the need for one."

She turned to her aunt. "Can I bring mine here if my daddy wants me to live with him?"

Autumn's eyes shot up to lock with his, a frown pulling at her glossy pink lips. "My sister's last request," she explained. "One I'm struggling to honor."

He hadn't even given that any thought. Tucker knelt in front of his daughter and took her tiny hand in his. "Of course, I want you to come live with me. I would've brought you here to live with me sooner if I had known about you." He looked to Autumn. "Thank you for bringing her home."

"Home is yet to be decided," she said stiffly. "I'm only here because my sister asked me to let you know about Blue. I'm not about to leave my niece in anyone else's care, not even yours, until I know in my heart that you're capable of doing right by her."

And he wasn't about to lose his daughter after only just finding her. "Understood," he answered with a nod, appreciating the protective stance she'd taken when it came to Blue. "But you should understand, too, that I intend to do whatever it takes to have my daughter in my life." Autumn Myers was about to learn that her niece's daddy was a man of his word. One worthy of the daughter the good Lord had blessed him with.

Autumn drew the quilt atop Tucker's guest bed up over her niece and then tucked it in snugly around her tiny form.

Blue gave a sleepy smile. "'Night, Aunt Autumn."

"Sleep tight, sweetie," she said, leaning in to kiss the top of Blue's head. Then she walked over to the suitcase she'd packed Blue's clothes in for their trip there. She'd chosen to bring a good week's worth of outfits, not knowing if they would be staying but deciding it was best to be prepared just in case. It seemed tonight, at least, they would be staying.

When Tucker had invited them into his home, even going so far as to fix them grilled cheese sandwiches because Blue had told him they hadn't eaten dinner yet, her niece had barely been able to keep her eyes open. Autumn had decided it best to call it a night and set up a time to meet with Tucker the following day. She'd had every intention of taking Blue to one of the nearby hotels she'd called before coming to Bent Creek to check on room availability, but Tucker had insisted they take one of his guest rooms.

When she'd politely refused Tucker's offer, not wanting to impose, he'd told her that his house was Blue's as well, and it was long past time she had a chance to stay there. He topped that statement off with a heartfelt *please* before adding that he intended to take himself out to the barn to sleep on the cot he'd set up a few weeks prior when he'd wanted to watch over one of his horses that had been under the weather at the time.

Not quite the actions of a selfish, responsibility-shirking cowboy, which she had believed him to be for the past five-plus years. He appeared to be quite the opposite. At least, when it came to first impressions. Tucker had accepted Blue into his life without a moment's hesitation, seemed more than willing to prove himself and had even offered to sleep in the barn to give them some privacy. All of that and a soft spot for animals. Throw in that rugged cowboy look that both she and Summer had always been drawn to, something Autumn had learned was best to avoid. What was there not to like? Other than the fact that Tucker Wade's very existence could mean a lifetime of heartache for her if Blue ended up being raised by her daddy.

Autumn busied herself with getting Blue's clothes ready for the next day, hoping to take her mind off the handsome cowboy who had managed to steal at least a piece of her sister's well-guarded heart.

"Does my daddy have horses?" Blue asked sleepily.

Her daddy. How odd those words sounded coming from her niece, Autumn thought, struggling not to frown. "I thought you were sleeping."

"I am," her niece replied. "Almost. Does he?"

"He does," she answered. "In fact, your daddy has a ranch filled with them." From what she'd learned, Tucker Wade and his brothers were stock contractors for rodeos, dealing specifically in the horses used for events like saddle bronc and bareback bronc riding. Apparently, Summer had been keeping tabs on her husband from afar, collecting news clippings, and even a detailed report from the private investigator her sister had hired the year before, unbeknownst to Autumn. They all showed a man who was hardworking, always willing to lend a hand to help those in need and a man of unbending faith. He'd retired from the rodeo circuit to run stock horses with his two brothers.

"But I didn't see any."

"Maybe because you were fast asleep when we pulled in. Besides, they were probably off running through the hills."

"I don't like horses."

While Autumn had never been as at ease around horses as Summer had, she didn't fear them like Blue did now. Her niece had always displayed the same passion for animals as her mother had. At least, until Summer's accident. Blue would spend hours on end out in the barn with her momma while Summer tended to Alamo, the eight-year-old quarter horse her sister had purchased that past year.

Having a horse of her own again had given Summer back some of that spark that had been missing since she'd had to sell her beloved Cinnamon, the horse she'd ridden during her barrel-racing days, to help pay for the cost of formula and diapers for Blue. Her daughter's needs had always come first with Summer. Unlike it had been with their own mother.

Autumn settled herself onto the edge of the mattress with a sad smile. "Your momma wouldn't want you to blame Alamo or any other horses for what happened. Snakes are very scary creatures, even to big, strong horses. Alamo just wanted to get away from it."

"I don't like snakes, either," Blue said with a yawn.

Autumn managed the semblance of a smile. "That makes two of us, sweetheart."

"I miss Momma."

Just shy of five years old, her niece should still have her mother in her life. The sadness in Blue's eyes whenever she spoke about missing her momma never failed to make Autumn's heart break.

"I know you do, sweetie," Autumn replied past the lump that had risen in her throat, still trying to come to terms with the recent loss of her sister herself. Summer had been gone for nearly six months and it still didn't seem real. Her twin, older than Autumn by mere minutes, had been called home to the Lord a week after being thrown from her horse.

"Are you gonna leave me, too?" her precious little Blue asked fearfully.

Autumn fought back an onslaught of tears. How was she supposed to answer that? Because if her sister's last wishes were carried out, she would be leaving Blue in the care of a man who hadn't even known his daughter existed.

"Not a chance," she heard herself reply. If this life-changing drive to Bent Creek, Wyoming, two counties away from Cheyenne, and the only home her niece had ever known, turned out the way Autumn hoped it would, her niece would be coming home with her for good. Despite the fact that she had been struggling since Summer's passing to place her complete faith in the Lord, Autumn sent up a silent prayer that she would be able to keep her promise to her sister if Tucker managed to prove himself worthy. In that case, she would make sure she stayed in her niece's life. Still, she couldn't even begin to imagine her life without Blue in it. Her niece was a living, breathing piece of Summer. All Autumn had left of her sister. And it was the love she had for her twin, as well as her not-quite-three-year-old niece— because that was all the older Blue was at the time—that had motivated Autumn to sell her real estate business in Braxton, Texas, where she and Summer had grown up, and move to Wyoming to be with them.

Blue turned onto her side, snuggling deeper under the blue-and-green-floral quilt. "Do you think my daddy liked our surprise?"

She had told Blue they were going to surprise her daddy with a visit and not to feel bad if he didn't seem happy about it, that some people didn't know how to handle surprises. Truth was she was preparing her niece in the kindest way she knew how for Tucker's possible rejection. If that had happened, Blue wouldn't feel the least bit unlovable. An emotion Autumn had experienced firsthand. But Tucker, though thoroughly shocked, had seemed to be overjoyed to learn that he had a daughter.

"How could he not when you're the surprise?" Autumn said, reaching out to stroke her niece's long curls.

With a sleepy smile, Blue closed her eyes and gave in to the exhaustion she'd been fighting.

Autumn closed her eyes as well, only not in sleep, but in one final prayer that night. *Dear Lord, please have a care with my niece's tender heart when Your will, whatever that may be, is done.*

Chapter Two

Autumn, cup of freshly brewed coffee in hand, moved to stand at the edge of the porch, her gaze skimming over the vast land around her. She loved all the warm colors that came with the fall season. The brilliant golds and vibrant reds with bold splashes of burgundy. The same colorful palette that now dotted the towering trees that surrounded Tucker Wade's ranch and filled the distant hills. Earthy shades of green and brown carpeted the ground below, making the colors in the trees above stand out even more.

Closing her eyes, she breathed in the cool, crisp air that filled the mornings at that time of year. Much to her surprise, a feeling of peacefulness settled over her as she stood in the faint chill of the early morning, listening to the faint sounds of nature stirring to life around her. It was a peacefulness she hadn't known for a very long while.

The unexpected calm that filled her at that moment took Autumn by surprise. Especially when one considered her reason for being there. Maybe it was a sign from God that everything was going to be all right. She'd certainly prayed hard enough. And there was no doubt in her mind that Blue was better off with her than with a man whose entire life centered around horses, whether it was riding them or getting them rodeo ready. Tucker Wade would have a very hard time convincing her otherwise.

Then again, what if this was the Lord's way of telling her that Bent Creek was the right place for her niece? That Blue would find contentment in this vast, horse-filled land hours from the only home she'd ever known.

No, Autumn thought in a panic, *the right place for Blue is back in Cheyenne with the one person who loves her more than anyone else ever could.* She had to believe that. Surely, the Lord knew that, as well. He'd seen the sacrifices Autumn had made for those she loved. For Blue.

That precious child filled her heart to overflowing. She didn't need a husband or even children of her own to make her happy. Not as long as she had Blue.

Not as long as she had Blue.

No sooner had that thought gone through her mind than the feeling of serenity that had come over her only moments before began to slip. In its place, the very real fear of losing her cherished little Blue Belle. A fear she'd been struggling with ever since Summer let loose the secrets she'd been keeping for so long. Secrets Autumn found herself wishing her sister would have taken with her to the grave.

Guilt filled her instantly at even harboring such a thought. Blue deserved to know her daddy, just as Tucker Wade deserved to know his little girl. They had both been denied the opportunity for far too long. Autumn couldn't let her own selfish needs and wants stop her from doing what was right. Doing what the Lord would want her to do.

"Morning."

Autumn jumped, her eyes flying open at the deep, baritone sound. Hot coffee sloshed over the rim of the cup she held clutched in her hand, causing her to wince.

Tucker Wade was there in an instant, standing on the other side of the porch's railing as he reached out to ease the cup from her stinging hand. "I didn't mean to startle you," he said apologetically as he set the coffee cup onto the railing a safe distance away. Then he pulled a red-and-white-print handkerchief from the back pocket of his jeans and handed it to her, asking worriedly, "You okay?"

She took the offered square of colorful cotton and dabbed at her hand. "I'm fine," she said with a half-hearted smile.

His gaze dropped to the red spots on her hand, and his frown deepened. "You need to run that hand under some cold water." Without waiting for a reply, he turned and made his way around to the side of the house, returning a moment later with a garden hose in hand. The water was coming out in a slow, gentle trickle. "Hold out that hand," he said.

"I really don't…" she began to protest, then seeing the determination on the cowboy's face had her saving her breath. Holding her hand out over the railing, she watched as Tucker Wade ran the cool water over the reddened patches of skin the spilled coffee had left behind.

"Better?" he asked, glancing up at her with a warm smile.

But the smile wasn't what drew and held her attention. It was his eyes. Slightly more brilliant than Blue's, she decided. A vivid shade of bright green. Like the heart-shaped leaves found on lemon clover. And those thick lashes…

"Autumn?"

She snapped out of her thoughts, her cheeks warming at having been so distracted by this man. So what if Tucker Wade had striking eyes and a kind smile? A handsome face had nothing to do with the man's ability to care for his daughter. She gave a quick nod. "Yes. Thank you."

"Glad to help." His smile widened into a teasing grin as he worked to shut off the hose's nozzle. "Maybe I should have suggested you help yourself to the orange juice in the fridge instead."

Her gaze touched briefly on the coffee cup atop the porch railing and then back to Tucker Wade. "I didn't sleep very well last night, so waking up to the aroma of freshly brewed coffee was a most welcomed thing." Not only had Tucker insisted she and Blue spend the night there instead of driving into town, he'd set the timer on his coffee maker so it would be ready for her when she awoke.

"That makes two of us," he admitted with a sigh.

"You should have slept in the house last night," she said with a frown.

"It had nothing to do with that," he assured her. "We cowboys are used to camping outdoors, so a cot in a barn isn't so bad. I just had a lot on my mind."

"Understandable." She glanced toward the sun that was slowly rising up from the distant horizon and then back to him. "At least Blue slept well last night," she said. "Not a single nightmare."

"You expected her to have bad dreams here?"

"I didn't know," she said honestly. "They happen on occasion. Ever since her momma died."

"Maybe the distraction of being in a new place will help to ease her nightmares."

"I pray it does." She glanced toward the rising sun and then back to Tucker. "So are you always up this early?"

"Earlier, usually," he replied. "I'm a bit off my game today."

She nodded in understanding. "The coffee's still hot if you'd like a cup," she offered. Despite his reassurances, she knew he couldn't have been very comfortable doing so with the nights getting so cold, but she appreciated his willingness.

"Coffee sounds good," he replied.

"Blue should be getting up soon. She's an early riser, but I expect her to be up even earlier this morning, considering this is her first breakfast with her daddy."

He glanced toward the front door, his expression one of nervous apprehension.

Autumn laughed softly. "It's not as if you're about to face a den of lions as Daniel once had to. Blue's a very sweet, loving little girl."

His gaze shifted back to her. "My little girl," he said as if in awe of the words that he'd just spoken, his voice choked with emotion. "And I don't have the slightest idea where to begin."

That admission couldn't be easy for a man like Tucker Wade. Cowboys were a proud lot. She should have been encouraged by his honesty, a sign that maybe he wasn't mentally prepared to raise a child. But she found herself offering him a reassuring smile. "I'd start with a 'good morning' once she wakes up and then prepare to answer a lot of questions. Everything from 'Are clouds made up of cotton balls?' to 'Why can't chickens fly?'"

Tucker chuckled.

"Laugh now," she warned playfully. "But don't say I didn't warn you once the questions begin. Your daughter can be very inquisitive."

"Duly noted."

"You cook?" she asked in surprise.

The corners of his mouth lifted, revealing a lone dimple. The same dimple her niece displayed with every smile. "A man's gotta eat." That said, he started off around the house, dragging the garden hose behind him. "Plain to see where Blue got her 'inquisitiveness' from," he called back over a broad shoulder before disappearing from sight.

The moment Autumn realized she was still smiling, she forced her mouth into a tight line. She would not, could not, like Tucker Wade. He was the enemy. The one person who could take away the only family she had left. Not waiting for Tucker, she grabbed for her cup of coffee and marched determinedly back into the house.

Hearing the front door to his ranch house close, Tucker took a moment to calm his racing thoughts. There were times as he'd stood talking to Autumn that he found himself thinking of Summer. How could he not? Autumn was the spitting image of his wife, except for having shorter hair and more of a businesslike style of dress. And she was every bit as pretty. Not at all surprising, considering they were identical twins. Yet, Autumn seemed different. Where his wife had always lived her life being her true self, her sister seemed more reserved; guarded, almost. Not that the situation they found themselves in didn't give her reason to be, but Tucker found himself wondering what she would be like with all those protective layers peeled away.

When Autumn had let down her guard for those brief moments that morning, allowing her more playful side to come out, she reminded him even more of her sister. But she wasn't Summer, the woman who had run out on him, taking with her a very huge part of him—his daughter.

His daughter. A lump formed in Tucker's throat, causing him to swallow hard. He was somebody's daddy. Blue's daddy. She was the most precious responsibility he'd ever been given. He knew nothing about raising children. She knew nothing about him. It felt as if he were going down a steep set of stairs in the dark with no handrail to hold on to. He didn't want to fall. Didn't want to fail. Not when God had chosen him to bestow this incredible blessing on.

Blue Belle Wade. Wait until his family found out about her. They'd be as shocked as he'd been. Even more so, seeing as how they had no idea he'd ever been married. So many things he would have done differently if given the chance. But there was no going back in life, only forward. And with that in mind, he intended to make it up to Blue for being absent from her life for so long, even if that absence hadn't been his choice.

Taking a deep breath, Tucker headed inside, closing the front door quietly behind him as he made his way to the kitchen. The coffee mug Autumn had been using sat on the kitchen table, but she was nowhere in sight. Crossing the kitchen, he grabbed himself a mug and filled it with coffee. Then he busied himself with starting breakfast for his guests.

Tucker caught himself, mentally changing that to for

his daughter and her aunt. His daughter was not a guest. She was family. *His family.* That thought had him whistling a happy tune as he moved about the kitchen.

"Care to tell us what's going on with you today?"

Speaking of family. Tucker turned to find Jackson and Garrett standing just inside the kitchen entryway, worried frowns on their faces. They'd clearly come before finishing up that morning's tasks.

"Everything okay with the horses?" he asked, worried that something might have happened with one. His brothers looked so serious.

"They're fine," Jackson replied. "It's you we're concerned about. You never call off when there's work to be done."

He'd spent a long, restless night, caught up in thoughts of his little girl. He'd also spent a good bit of time praying for the Lord to give him the strength to find it in himself to forgive Summer as Autumn had, because at that moment the depth of her betrayal was still too fresh to get past the simmering resentment he felt inside.

"Judging by the happy little tune you were whistling when we came in," Garrett said, "I'm guessing you're not under the weather."

"No," Tucker replied, feeling guilty for causing his brothers unnecessary worry. He hadn't made mention of Blue when he'd called to let them know he wouldn't be meeting up with them at the main barn that morning, because that was the kind of news he preferred to give them in person. "I'm not under the weather."

His oldest brother's frown deepened. "That being the case, care to let us in on what's really going on with you, then?"

Where did he begin? Tucker sent a quick prayer heavenward for some guidance from the Lord in the best way to handle this situation. One that affected him as well as his family. "I—"

"You're really tall," a tiny voice stated, cutting into Tucker's response.

His gaze shot between his brothers to see Blue standing there in the living room, looking up at Garrett and Jackson with youthful curiosity. She was wearing a long flannel nightgown covered in bright pink butterflies. Matching pink kitten heads peeked out from under the ruffled hem of her nightgown. A stuffed rag doll that looked as though it had gotten most of the stuffing loved right out of it drooped from her tiny hand.

His brothers' eyes widened in unison at the unexpected interruption before they pivoted on booted heels to look down at Blue. For the first time since Tucker could remember, his big brothers were rendered utterly speechless.

"Come on into the kitchen, sweetheart," he told his daughter, whose gaze was still fixed on her suddenly mute uncles.

Jackson and Garrett parted to let her through, their attention doing a slingshot in his direction as she passed by with a sleepy smile.

"Morning, Daddy," she said in the sweetest little singsong voice he'd ever heard. Her words grabbed at his heart. He was somebody's daddy, something he'd never expected to be after Summer had run out on their marriage. Not only had he been too hurt to think about trusting in love again, but also his still being legally wed to Summer had been keeping him from giving another relationship a chance.

Tucker returned his baby girl's smile, an unfamiliar warmth seeping into his heart as he did so. Then he placed his hands on her tiny shoulders and slowly turned her to face his brothers. "Blue Belle Wade, these two hulking giants who don't seem to be able to pick their jaws up from the kitchen floor are your uncles. That's your uncle Jackson on the left and your uncle Garrett on the right." He glanced down at his daughter, recalling she was only four. "Do you know what left and right are?"

She held out her hand, making and L shape with her fingers. "This is my left because left starts with *L*."

"Very good," he praised. He didn't know enough about children to say for sure, but something told him Blue was an extremely bright child.

"Uncles?" Jackson muttered in confusion as he stared at Blue.

Tucker looked up at his brother with an answering nod.

Garrett attempted to process what he'd just heard. "Blue Belle Wade?" he repeated slowly, his gaze fixed on Blue with her bright smile and reddish-brown curls.

"My daughter," Tucker said, still trying to come to grips with it all himself.

Garrett's wide-eyed gaze snapped up to Tucker. "Your what?"

"His daughter," Blue announced proudly, her tiny chin lifting.

"Daughter?" Jackson repeated, understandably confused by Blue's announcement.

"Who's hungry?" Tucker said with forced calm. He didn't want his brothers' raised voices to startle his daughter. "We can talk more about this while we eat. I'm making bacon and eggs."

Blue's gleeful expression fell. "But Aunt Autumn always makes me pancakes."

"I'm making pancakes, too," Tucker promptly amended, causing his brother's gazes to swing sharply in his direction.

Jackson snorted. "Since when do you make pancakes?"

"He's not," another female voice chimed in. "I am."

His brothers stepped aside as Autumn made her way past them into the kitchen to stand beside him and Blue.

This wasn't how he'd envisioned this moment to go. He hadn't even had a chance to prepare his brothers for the shock of finding out they were uncles. "I don't have a pancake mix," Tucker admitted guiltily.

"The best pancakes are made from scratch anyways," Autumn said with a smile and then leaned over to speak to Blue. "Sweetie, I thought I told you to wait for me in the bathroom while I grabbed your hairbrush and ponytail holder from your suitcase and a change of clothes."

"I was hungry."

"Even so, you shouldn't be wandering around by yourself."

"I wasn't by myself," she said, looking up at Tucker who stood on her other side. "I was with my daddy."

A slight frown tugged at Autumn's lips as she straightened. "Yes, I suppose you were."

Tucker looked over to find Garrett and Jackson staring at Autumn, mouths agape. And he understood why. They'd known Summer from the rodeo, had known their little brother had been sweet on her that rodeo season. And with Blue calling him daddy he could just imagine what they were thinking. Only they had it all wrong.

Clearing his throat, he said, "Jackson and Garrett, I'd like you to meet Autumn Myers, Summer's twin sister."

"Her twin?" Jackson said as if having trouble accepting that this wasn't the Summer they had once known, standing there.

"Identical twin," Autumn supplied with a sad smile.

Tucker wanted to explain why his wife wasn't there and her sister was, but he didn't want to mention Summer's passing with his daughter standing there. Her mother's loss had been traumatic enough for her as it was.

"My mommy's in heaven," Blue said sadly.

Tucker's heart ached for his little girl. No child should ever have to speak those words.

An uncomfortable silence fell over the room.

Clearing the emotion from his throat, Tucker said, "Her aunt Autumn brought Blue here to meet her family."

"And maybe I'll get to live here if you want me," Blue reminded him.

"As I said before, wanting you isn't an issue," he replied tenderly. "I do without a doubt. You belong here."

"Tucker, please," Autumn warned in a hushed voice beside him. "Don't get her hopes up. It's too soon."

"*You* have a daughter," Garrett said disbelievingly.

Tucker nodded. "I do."

"All these years and you've never said anything?" Jackson grumbled, clearly hurt by what he thought had been Tucker's decision to keep Blue's existence from them.

"Why don't Blue and I give you men a few moments of privacy while she gets dressed for the day?" Autumn said, taking her niece by the hand. "Just give me a holler when you're ready for me to start on those pancakes."

His brothers parted to let them through.

"Are my uncles mad at my daddy?" Tucker heard Blue ask as Autumn led her away. Any answer her aunt might have given was lost as the two scurried toward the entryway.

Garrett waited a moment and then turned to face him. "I can't believe you kept this from us."

Tucker hated the censure he saw in his brother's eyes.

Jackson crossed the room to grab a couple of coffee cups from the cupboard. "I wouldn't have expected this from you," he muttered as he placed them onto the counter and then reached for the coffeepot. "Momma raised us better than that."

This was going to be even harder than he'd imagined it would be, not that he'd had much time to think about how everything was going to play out. Just one sleepless night in the barn. He took a seat at the table and dragged a hand down over his face, feeling the stubble of his unshaven jaw. "I didn't know about Blue," he said, the admission stoking the flames of his resentment toward Summer for keeping his daughter from him. "Not until last evening when Autumn showed up on my doorstep to tell me about Summer's…passing." The word caught in his throat.

"I'm sorry," Garrett said solemnly. "I know how much she meant to you at one time."

Enough to marry, Tucker thought, his jaw tightening.

Jackson walked over and handed Garrett a steaming mug and then both men settled themselves into the empty chairs across the table from Tucker, disapproval etched into their tanned faces.

"I know what you're both thinking," Tucker grumbled. "And you're wrong."

"You just told us that Blue is your daughter," their oldest brother said, pinning Tucker with his gaze.

"She is. Only I didn't know Summer was carrying my child when she walked away from our marriage."

Jackson nearly choked on the sip of coffee he'd just taken. "Marriage?"

"You both know I fell pretty hard for her when we met. By the time rodeo season came to an end, I couldn't imagine leaving her. She felt the same." At least, he'd thought she had. But if she had, she would have told him about the baby. Would have given him the chance to think about giving up the rodeo life, instead of making the decision herself to end something they had started together. "We both decided to put down roots in Cheyenne, the place where we'd first met. So I bought her a ring and got married at the courthouse."

"You have something against church weddings?" Garrett asked with a disapproving frown.

"We wanted a quick, small, private wedding."

"Can't get more private than a courthouse wedding," Jackson muttered angrily as he brought his coffee cup to his lips. "You might have at least included your immediate family in something as sacred as the exchanging of your wedding vows."

Garrett's downturned mouth pulled tighter. "And to think we all believed you had stayed behind when rodeo season ended to work a job until the next year's circuit began anew."

He had found filler work in Cheyenne to help pay the bills. That much was true.

"Did your rushed marriage have something to do with Summer having your baby?"

Tucker pinned his oldest brother with his gaze. "Blue

came after the fact. I rushed into a hasty marriage with Summer because I was young and thought love was something it turned out not to be," he replied, feeling the need to clarify things.

"We all knew you were always one to jump feet-first into the fire," Garrett said crossly, "but marriage, Tucker? Never mind the not including us when the nuptials took place, because you and I both know I would have done my best to talk you out of it with you being only twenty-four at the time. But why not tell us about your marriage afterward?"

"Summer and I agreed to take a little time to settle into marriage before telling our families. My family actually," he amended, "as my wife led me to believe she had none. But things changed. My wife changed." He went on to tell his brothers everything he knew, but there were still so many unanswered questions he might never get answers to now that she was gone.

Empathy replaced the hurt and anger he'd seen in Garrett's eyes. His brother released a heavy sigh. "I'm sorry you had to go through that. It certainly explains why you've avoided any real relationship since that summer. I put it off to your not wanting the distraction while competitively riding. Then after we started up our rodeo stock company I thought it had something to do with your delving hard into that. Never in a million years would I have guessed the truth having anything to do with you being married."

Jackson sat back against the kitchen chair and shoved a splayed hand back through his thick hair. "I still can't process the fact that my baby brother is a married man."

"Widowed," Tucker said flatly. Then, fighting back the emotion that had been roiling around in his gut all morning, he said, "And it was my forgiveness she should have been seeking at the end."

"There's no denying that Summer did you wrong," Jackson acknowledged with a frown. "But she did right by asking the Lord for forgiveness. If you were there, then maybe—"

"But I wasn't," Tucker ground out, cutting his brother off. "I didn't even know where *there* was. She left without so much as a goodbye and never made any attempt to contact me, or let me know where she was. At some point, she came back to Cheyenne, but I must have already moved back home."

"It's possible she tried to find you at some point, but you were already gone," Garrett said hopefully.

"Summer knew I was born and raised in Bent Creek. She could have found me easy enough. But my wife chose to keep my little girl from me." A myriad of emotions filled him at that moment, feelings he didn't know how to deal with.

His brothers exchanged worried glances and then Garrett said, "It's going to be okay."

"How?" Tucker demanded. "I've missed so much. My daughter's first smile. Her first steps. Her first birthday." Shoving away from the table, he crossed the room to stand at the sink, staring out the bay window that looked out over the back pasture. "I'm her father," he said, his voice breaking, "and I don't even know when my daughter's birthday is."

Chairs scooted back from the kitchen table and then heavy-booted footsteps crossed the wood planks that made up the kitchen floor. A second later, he was bookended by his older brothers.

Garrett clasped a hand over his shoulder. "I can't even

begin to imagine what you're feeling right now, but I do know that the Lord has seen fit to bless our family with your little girl. And while we can't change the past, and the time we've lost with her, we can set our sights on the time we're going to have with Blue in the years to come."

Jackson nodded. "Garrett's right. What really matters is seeing to it that Blue is happy. We've got the rest of her life to celebrate her birthdays and holidays, and worship together."

If only it were that simple. "I pray that's how it goes," he replied. "First, I have to prove myself capable of caring for Blue to her aunt. Autumn has custody of my daughter, and, while she's here honoring her sister's wishes, she's made it perfectly clear she's not going to simply turn her niece over to me."

"Then you'll prove yourself capable," Jackson said determinedly. "All of us will."

Garrett looked to them both. "Good plan, but care to tell me how we do that when none of us have the slightest idea of how to care for a child, let alone a little girl?"

"Looks like I'm going to have to call Mom sooner than I'd planned," Tucker said with a sigh. "I'd hoped to wait a few days until I'd had a chance to come to terms with suddenly being somebody's daddy."

"Don't," Jackson said with a frown. "They've wanted to go on this trip for as long as I can remember. What's a few more weeks?"

Tucker shook his head. "It can't wait. I won't lose Blue." If it came down to it, he'd fight for her legally. But a legal battle wasn't something he wanted to put his daughter through. So that left proving himself to Autumn.

"You won't," Jackson said with conviction. "We'll figure something out."

Garrett nodded in agreement.

Tucker glanced toward the doorway. "We'll talk more later. Right now, my little girl is eagerly awaiting pancakes."

"See there," Garrett said with a grin, "you're already stepping into daddy mode."

Jackson slapped Tucker on the back. "All I can say is better you than me. I'm nowhere ready to settle down to that kind of responsibility yet. However, I am looking forward to being Blue's favorite uncle."

"You're going to have to settle for second favorite," Garrett told him as they made their way out of the kitchen. "I have access to kittens."

"Using your job to win her over," Jackson grumbled. "That's low. Guess I'll have to break out the friendship card and take Blue to Sandy's Candy's." Sandy was a classmate of Jackson's who made the best homemade fudge in the county. But she also had counters filled with assorted sweets, including an entire section of penny candies.

Tucker felt some of the worry that had been pressing down on him since awakening that morning lift away. He would make this work and be the father Blue deserved, because he wasn't in this alone. He had his family there to support him, to help Blue settle into what would be her new life. And, most important, he had the Lord to turn to when things got tough.

Chapter Three

"Are my uncles coming for pancakes today?"

Tucker looked to Blue who was seated across the table from him next to her aunt Autumn. A large lace bow now held her curls in place as they trailed down her back in a neat ponytail. She'd changed out of her nightgown and into a fancy ruffled dress. "Not today, sweetheart."

"Don't they like pancakes?" she asked with a worried frown.

He could understand why she might think that. His brothers hadn't stuck around the morning before after discovering they had a niece partially because they felt they needed to give Tucker some time alone with his "guests." But he knew, having experienced the same shock of discovering Blue's existence, that Garrett and Jackson probably needed a little time to process everything. "Your uncles have to check on the horses and see to a few fence repairs."

"I don't like horses," Blue said with a frown, a sticky drop of pancake syrup clinging to her tiny chin.

Tucker's smile sagged with his daughter's announcement. How could a child conceived by two parents whose lives had once revolved solely around horses dislike them? More important, how was he supposed to see to it that his daughter was happy there at the ranch when she had an aversion to the very thing that put food on the table for his family? *Her* family.

Autumn picked up her napkin, dipped it into her water glass and then dabbed at the sticky syrup that had dribbled down Blue's chin. "Sweetie, we talked about this on the way here. You can't blame Alamo for what happened."

"Alamo?" he asked as he watched the ease with which Summer's sister cared for his daughter.

"Mommy's horse," Blue replied as she stabbed at another piece of syrup-laced pancake.

"The horse she was riding the day of the accident," Autumn explained as she set the damp paper napkin down next to her plate. "She hadn't owned Alamo all that long, so she had no way of knowing how he would react to being spooked. I have to imagine that most horses would be a little shaken up by a snake in their path."

He nodded. "Some horses tend to be afraid of snakes. Some aren't." His horse wasn't, but Hoss knew enough to give a snake a wide berth if they happened to cross paths. Same went with Little Joe, his more recently acquired saddle horse. "If only she'd been riding Cinnamon," he muttered with a frown. "He'd never been prone to spooking." One of the best quarter horses he'd come across in both manner and spirit.

"There have been far too many if onlys in our lives lately," Autumn responded with a sigh, her gaze shifting to Blue. Then she looked back to Tucker, a hint of something that could only be described as condemnation in her eyes. "She had to sell Cinnamon after Blue was born."

"Why?" he asked, unable to comprehend his wife ever parting with her beloved horse.

Autumn's pretty mouth twisted in a sign of irritation and one slender brow lifted.

"Babies take money, Mr. Wade," Autumn pointed out. "Medical bills, diapers, formula. Then there's childcare, because as a single parent, Summer had no choice but to work to keep a roof over their heads. So, as you see, my sister had no choice but to sell her horse."

Was she attempting to point blame in his direction for the difficulty Summer had gone through? Because it felt an awful lot like she was. "She had a choice," he said with forced calmness. He might not know much about raising children, but he knew enough to keep adult issues between adults. "I'd be more than happy to discuss it with you further at a more appropriate time," he said with a nod toward Blue, who seemed totally oblivious to the conversation going on around her. Her interest lay in swiping up every bit of the remaining syrup on her plate with her fingertip.

As if just realizing what she was doing, Autumn reached once more for her damp napkin. "Sweetie, it's not polite to lick the syrup off your finger." Taking his daughter's hand in hers, she proceeded to wipe it clean.

Blue's tiny mouth fell into a pout. "But I get to lick cotton candy off my fingers. And icing. And—"

"That's different," Autumn replied, a hint of frustration in her voice. She set the napkin down and stood, collecting both hers and Blue's plates and forks. "You're still sticky," she told her as she turned and started for the sink. "Why don't you run on into the bathroom and wash your hands with soap and water while I do up these dishes?"

"There's no need for you to do that," Tucker countered, his thoughts still dwelling on the fact that she blamed him for Summer's having to struggle financially.

Blue shifted in her chair, her gaze trailing after her aunt. "Can we go pick flowers afterward?"

Autumn shook her head. "It's October, sweetie. Not a very good time of year to be searching for flowers."

It was good to see his daughter had a fondness for the outdoors. After having spent the previous day stuck inside thanks to a sudden drop in temperature that preceded a brief thunderstorm that rolled in, Tucker looked forward to showing her around the ranch. Not that he had minded getting to know his baby girl while playing dozens of games of Go Fish and Old Maid. Autumn had spent some of that time making work calls, and the rest observing the two of them. Until he proved himself, he had no choice but to accept that everything he did was going to be under Autumn's close scrutiny.

"Actually," Tucker said, "I happen to know where we can find some yellow rabbitbrush in bloom."

Blue's face lit up. "I like yellow!"

"Don't you have to help your brothers with those repairs today?" Autumn asked.

He shook his head. "Jackson called this morning to tell me they were going to focus on the two worst sections of the fence line today and see to the rest tomorrow. Garrett has a few vet calls he needs to make today, which means I'm free to take Blue out to find those flowers after breakfast."

Blue straightened in her chair, beaming excitedly. "Yay! Can we go now?"

* * *

Autumn smiled. "I'll get you ready as soon as I finish cleaning up the kitchen."

Tucker nodded. "I'll give you a hand with these breakfast dishes. Then I'll go grab a quick shower before we go look for those blooms. That is, if it's all right with your aunt Autumn."

Blue swung her gaze around. "Can my daddy get a shower before we go for a ride?"

"Yes." Autumn wasted no time in responding, a grin parting her pink lips. "He may."

"That's not what I meant," he muttered, a flash of heat spreading through his whiskered cheeks.

A snort of laughter passed through Autumn's curved lips, drawing his attention in her direction. He couldn't help but notice how pretty she was when she wasn't scowling at him with condemnation. Her humor-filled gaze met his. "For future reference, children take almost everything that is said quite literally."

"I'll be sure to keep that in mind."

She looked to Blue. "What Tucker...that is, your daddy," she promptly corrected, "meant to say was that he needs to make sure your going for a ride with him would be all right with me."

"The invitation was for the both of you," Tucker clarified.

"Oh," Autumn said, as if surprised by his wanting to include her. "I thought—"

"You've thought a lot of things about me that I hope to have a chance to set to rights," he said determinedly.

"Can we go?" Blue pleaded, her face alight with excitement. "Please, Aunt Autumn!"

Autumn looked to Tucker. "I'd hate to—"

"Don't say *impose*," he told her as he stood to carry his own dishes over to the sink. "I want to show the two of you around. Give Blue an idea of what it will be like to live here at the Triple W Rodeo Ranch."

"*If* she lives here," Autumn immediately countered as if he'd forgotten her telling him he had to prove himself before she'd turn care of Blue over to him. Care he rightfully should have been a part of from the beginning.

"Rest assured my daughter will be with me." He'd lost too much precious time with Blue as it was thanks to Summer.

"Do yellow rabbits live in the flower bush?"

His gaze still locked with Autumn's, he said in confusion, "Yellow rabbits?"

A semblance of a smile returned once more to her pretty face. "I did warn you to prepare yourself for this. And now you have a perfect example of a four-year-old's never-ending and sometimes completely unexpected questions." She turned to Blue. "Sweetie, there is no such thing as a yellow rabbit."

"But I ate one at Easter."

Tucker's brow lifted.

"Real rabbits don't have bright yellow fur," Autumn went on to explain to his daughter. "Only candy bunnies do." She turned to him, explaining further, "She's referring to marshmallow Peeps."

How did she get all of that out of his daughter's question? Did the ability to decipher a child's way of thinking just come naturally for some, or was it something one learned over time? He prayed it was the latter, because it clearly wasn't instinctive for him. Autumn's clarification had made things clearer on his end, however.

He turned to Blue, who was watching them from

where she remained seated at the table. "They call it yellow rabbitbrush because the yellow flowers that grow on them are a favorite treat of jackrabbits."

"Oh," his daughter said with a sigh, sounding disappointed.

If he could have, he would have covered the bushes they were going to see in marshmallow bunnies. But those edible delights were somewhat scarce in October. However, he had something else up his sleeve that he was fairly sure his daughter would be just as excited over.

"We might even stop by your grandma and grandpa's place to collect some eggs from the chickens in their henhouse on the way home."

"I have a grandma and grandpa?" she squeaked excitedly.

"You sure do," he said with a grin. "They're not home right now because they're on a trip but you'll get to meet them very soon."

"Do their chickens live in a house like yours?"

"A much smaller version," he answered with a chuckle. "Now scoot and get those hands washed up, or you're going to end up with chicken feathers sticking to your fingers."

With a giggle, she hopped down and raced from the kitchen.

He looked to Autumn. "You might want to have her change into a pair of jeans."

"Blue loves her dresses," she said, slender brows drawing together in what appeared to be irritation at his request. "Most little girls do. And if you're trying to make her into something she's not—"

"We're going on a hike," he reminded her. "With plants and trees and rocky ground. Probably not the best conditions for that pretty little dress she's wearing. But since you are her legal guardian, it's your call."

"Oh, I'm sorry," she said with a sigh. "I thought you were trying to..." Her words trailed off as she searched for what Tucker assumed was a less accusatory explanation.

"Turn her into a cowgirl?" he supplied.

She lowered her gaze guiltily.

"Considering she's mine and Summer's," he continued, "that's bound to come naturally. But I won't force my daughter to be someone she doesn't want to be when she comes to live here."

Her averted gaze snapped up to lock with his. "That transition, should it come at all, will be done in a slow, well-thought-out manner to assure Blue suffers no long-term emotional trauma from being uprooted from the only life she's ever known."

What about the emotional trauma that had been done to him? But this wasn't about his issues. It was about what was best for his little girl. He understood Autumn's reluctance to turn over custody of her niece after being such an integral part of his daughter's life, but this was something he wasn't backing down from. "I agree we need to make the transition for Blue as smooth as possible, but you need to start preparing yourself, as well. My daughter *will* be in my life and I'm not referring to brief holiday visits."

"I could drag things out in court if it came down to it," she replied.

"But you won't."

She shook her head, and with a resigned sigh said, "No. I wouldn't put her through that. If you prove capable of taking care of my niece, I will put my trust in the Lord to watch over her when I'm not here to do so.

However, my niece *will* be in my life," she said, repeating his earlier words. "And *I'm* not referring to brief holiday visits."

"I wouldn't have it any other way," he said honestly, admiring her fire when it came to protecting Blue. "My daughter is your family, too. Is that what you're worked up about? That possibility that I'll cut you out of her life?"

She turned away.

"Autumn, I wasn't the one who walked away from my marriage. Summer was." He frowned. "I'll be the first to admit that we were both too young to really know what we were getting into, but I would've done my best to make things work between us if she had only given me a chance. Baby and all."

Her shoulders shuddered, and he knew by her silence that she was fighting back tears.

"Autumn…" he said, reaching out to place a comforting hand on her shoulder. He understood her pain. She had already lost her sister. She feared losing Blue as well, something he would never do to her.

She held up a hand, but remained standing as she was. "I'm okay. A little worse for wear after a lot of sleepless nights, but I'll pull it together."

Her conviction was strong, and he imagined she would do just that. Autumn seemed to have an inner strength his wife had never quite mastered. Hers was carefully controlled. Her decisions well-thought-out, where her sister hadn't always taken the time to consider the effect her words or her actions might have had on those around her.

He forced himself to let his hand fall away, but he remained where he was. "I can only imagine how hard this has been on you. Losing your sister that way. Suddenly having to take on the responsibility of raising her child. Not to mention the financial burden…"

She turned to face him. The thick tears looming in her light blue eyes made them appear as if they were liquid silver. "There wasn't anything sudden about it. I gave up the real estate business I had built up back home in Lone Tree to come to Wyoming and help my sister with her little girl, both emotionally and financially, long before the Lord called Summer home. I found part-time work as a Realtor, planning my appointments around Summer's waitressing job so one of us could be home with Blue at all times. Everything was perfect until…" A sob caught in her throat.

His heart ached for this woman who had dedicated so much of her life to caring for his daughter. "They were blessed to have you."

"No," she countered without hesitation. "*I* was blessed to have them. They filled an emptiness I had inside me that I never knew was there." Her teary gaze drifted toward the empty doorway. "That little girl is everything to me. I love her with all my heart and I will do right by her." Her teary gaze returned to him. "So, natural father or not, you're gonna have to climb a very high mountain to reach the point where I feel she'd be better off with you than with myself and the life she already has in Cheyenne."

She'd already made that point quite clear, but he wisely kept that thought to himself. She had a right to feel the way she did. He was a stranger. A man who she had believed for years had done her sister wrong. And while he was the one who had truly been ill-treated, he intended to put his all into winning Autumn over. She deserved that much, knowing now the selfless sacrifices she'd made in her own life to make Blue's better.

"Whatever it takes," he said softly, fighting the urge to brush away a stray tear from her cheek. At that moment, she looked weary and vulnerable. Not at all like the lioness protecting her cub that he'd seen her be.

"I should go check on Blue."

"Make sure you both wear comfortable shoes," he called out as she started from the kitchen. "We'll be hiking up a trail that has bits of stone scattered about it to get to the flowers I promised to show Blue."

"We will." She paused in the doorway and cast a glance back over her shoulder. "Thank you for including me." Before Tucker could reply, she was gone.

Autumn sat quietly, looking out the passenger-side window of Tucker's truck as he drove them across his property. Not that she would have had a chance to say much with her niece chattering away from her car seat behind them. Tucker's warm, husky laughter told her he didn't mind Blue's constant barrage of questions and comments one bit. In fact, and much to her dismay, he was doing and saying all the right things where his daughter was concerned, and Blue was eating her daddy's attention right up.

"I didn't think you had any nieces or nephews," Autumn muttered with a glance his way. That was the only thing that could explain his comfort level around Blue. Yet, Summer hadn't mentioned Blue having any cousins on Tucker's side.

He shook his head. "I don't. My brothers are as single as they come, with no plans to settle down anytime soon."

She frowned at his reply. That meant Tucker was just

a natural with children. She should have known that by how quickly her niece had taken to him.

"I take it one of my brothers caught your interest this morning."

The question was so unexpected, Autumn found herself choking. "What?" She turned to find him attempting to smother a grin, that lone Wade dimple that Tucker and both of his brothers had inherited in the family gene pool etched deep into his tanned cheek.

He cast a quick glance in her direction. "You looked a little put out to hear that my brothers are committed bachelors," he explained, his gaze shifting back to the road, or, in their case, the pasture ahead.

Confusion must have lit her features, because he added, "You frowned when I made mention of their firm commitment to bachelorhood."

"What's interest?" Blue piped up from the back seat of the extended cab.

Autumn cast a disapproving glare his way. Leave it to her niece to lose interest in the scenery outside just when Tucker had made his offhanded comment. "Children miss nothing," she reminded him.

"I see that," he said, that devastatingly handsome grin still intact.

She had no doubt that his smile was what had first drawn her sister to this man. Rugged good looks aside, it was that playful curve of his lips with that lone-dimpled grin, one that exuded both humor and confidence and put others at ease, which was nearly irresistible. *Nearly.* But Tucker Wade was the enemy. At least as far as she was concerned, he was. The man was stealing Blue's affection away with his silly jokes and eagerness to go that extra mile to make his daughter happy.

"Will you look at that?" Tucker announced, pointing toward a sparsely wooded hillside a short distance ahead, one made up of a few scattered pines, dirt, rocks and splotches of dried-up grass.

"What?" Blue said excitedly, tipping sideways in an attempt to see out the front window of Tucker's truck, her view mostly blocked by the passenger seat Autumn was in.

Glancing up at Blue in the rearview mirror, Tucker smiled. "The rabbitbrush is just over the top of that hillside."

Autumn gasped, her head snapping around in his direction. "Are you telling me you intend to drive us up that mountain?"

Tucker chuckled. "It's a hill, not a mountain. And a poor excuse of a hill at that."

"When it involves my niece's safety, it might as well be a mountain," she said sharply.

"I would never do anything to risk her safety," he said with a frown. Tucker slowed the truck, coming to a stop along the foot of the hillside. "We'll leave the truck here and walk the rest of the way."

Her skeptical gaze shifted, taking in the rocky outcrop before them.

"It's easier than it looks," he assured her.

"I think it would be better if we made our way back to the house," she argued, feeling far less confident than Tucker was about the ease at which they'd be able to traverse the *hill*.

"But I wanna see the yellow rabbits," Blue whined.

"You won't see any yellow rabbits," Autumn reminded her niece. "Only yellow flowers."

"I'm hoping she'll get to see more than that," Tucker

stated as he cut the engine. He turned in the seat, his green eyes meeting hers. "Trust me."

Trust him? She didn't even know him. But there was something about Tucker Wade that made her feel she could do just that. Trusting a man didn't come easy for her. The last time she'd placed her trust completely in a man, he'd trampled all over it. Her heart, as well.

"Please?" Blue joined in, drawing Autumn back from her thoughts of the past.

A soft sigh passed through Autumn's lips. "Okay, we'll give it a try. But if the trail gets to be too much for Blue—"

"I'll carry her," Tucker said matter-of-factly.

Her gaze slid down to his strong arms. He could probably carry the both of them up that rather large hill if he had a mind to.

"You, too, if need be," he added, causing her gaze to snap back up to his grinning face.

Had she voiced her thoughts aloud? She hoped not.

"I really want Blue to see this," he added determinedly.

Autumn cleared her throat and looked away. "I'm perfectly capable of hiking up a hill." Not that she could remember the last time she'd done so.

With a nod, he opened the driver's side door and stepped down. "The offer still stands should you have need of it," he said with that irresistible boyish grin of his before shutting the door behind him.

Much to her chagrin, Autumn found herself grinning, too. She immediately wiped it away. She couldn't let Tucker Wade and his charming cowboy smile get under her skin. Not only for her niece's sake, but for her own. This man made her feel at ease in a way she hadn't allowed herself to be around a man for a very long time. Not since she was a naive eighteen-year-old who thought she'd met "the one."

Parker Booth, a Texas cowboy every bit as smooth talking as this Wyoming one, had known all the right things to say. Had made her feel like she was the most special girl in the world with his sugary words. They'd dated all summer, and Autumn was certain she had found "the one." A week before she was to leave for college, Parker let it slip that it was her fun-loving, barrel-racing twin he had really wanted. Only Summer hadn't reciprocated his feelings, so he figured Autumn was the next best thing. Tender heart broken, and refusing to be any man's second choice, Autumn had ended things with Parker, and sworn off cowboys altogether.

"This is supposed to be a fun outing," Tucker Wade's deep voice rumbled close to Autumn's ear.

She jumped, startled from her thoughts, and then looked up at Tucker. "I never said it wasn't."

"That expression you were wearing on your face a moment ago pretty much said it for you."

"This outing isn't about my enjoyment," she said, because admitting the real reason behind her frown wasn't something she intended to share with anyone. Even Summer hadn't known the truth about why Autumn only dated business professionals. She would have felt somehow responsible for the hurt Autumn had experienced. So while Summer dated ranch hands and rodeo cowboys, Autumn only went out with career-focused businessmen. Men who were not her type. Men she knew she'd never risk having her heart broken by. Men unlike Tucker Wade. It seemed she and her sister weren't so different after all.

"That's where you're wrong," Tucker said as they started walking again. "But I'll let you decide for yourself once we get there."

They continued working their way up and around the somewhat wooded, rocky hillside with Blue chattering away, her busy conversation directed to no one in particular. The trail was decently wide and free of the larger rocks and prickly shrubs and trees that littered the incline on either side of them. It was also a much easier hike than Autumn had first thought it would be. The air was brisk, but it felt good to be outside doing something physical, having spent most of her time indoors with Blue or in her office at work.

"Owie," Blue yelped suddenly, her hurried steps halting.

Autumn nearly tripped over her niece, Blue's stop had been so abrupt.

Tucker stepped around Autumn, concern etched in his tanned face. "Blue? What's wrong?"

"I got a rock in my shoe," her niece replied with a tiny pout. "A real big one."

He clicked his tongue as he knelt in front of his daughter. "Those pesky rocks. Always trying to sneak back up to the top of the hill in someone's shoe."

Autumn watched in silence as Tucker lifted his little girl with ease and settled her atop his bent leg. Her niece who was normally on the shy side around men, no doubt from having spent most of her life around her momma and Aunt Autumn, had taken so easily to Tucker. She wanted a daddy. Just like all the other children she knew had.

Tucker smoothed back a tendril of reddish-brown, baby-fine hair from Blue's face. "What do you say we have your aunt Autumn take a look?" he suggested, his tone low and soothing. One she imagined he used when one of his horses needed to be gentled.

Blue gave a tiny nod and then stuck her leg out.

Autumn brushed a couple of stones from the path before settling onto her knees in front of them. "We'll just shake those troublesome little stones right on out of there," she said with a tender smile as she untied and then slipped Blue's tennis shoe from her foot. Turning it over, she gave it a small shake, sending two offending pebbles back to the ground below.

"All gone," she said as she slid the sparkly, cotton-candy-pink tennis shoe back onto Blue's foot. Then she promptly worked its rainbow-colored shoestrings back into a neat bow. When she looked up, she found Tucker's green eyes watching her with a mixture of curiosity and something she couldn't quite put words to. And then he smiled, that lone dimple cutting deep into his tanned cheek. The effect that single gesture had on her was unsettling.

It would be easy to blame the unexpected quickening of her heartbeat to be the result of their brief hike up the hill, but she had never been one for mistruths—even to herself. Springing to her feet, Autumn took a hurried step back, her boot skidding on the miniscule pieces of stone that covered the trail.

Tucker was on his feet in an instant, Blue firmly ensconced in one arm as he reached out to steady her. "Careful there," he said in a low rumble. "Don't want you twisting an ankle."

She was normally very alert, but Tucker Wade was so... She struggled to find the right words, finally settling for *thoroughly distracting*. This man, no matter how charming or handsome, was her niece's daddy. Reason enough to fight this pull he seemed to have on her senses. But even more troubling was the fact that he had been her sister's husband. The last man on Earth she should ever find herself attracted to.

Keeping her gaze averted, Autumn managed a quick, "Thank you."

"No thanks necessary," Tucker replied as he bent to set his daughter back on her feet.

Blue clung to his neck, refusing to be put down. "I think you need to carry me."

"Blue," Autumn gently admonished.

"That so?" Tucker said with a chuckle, making no attempt to free himself of the adorable little burr clinging to him.

She nodded. "So no more rocks try to sneak up the hill in my shoe. Their family would miss them if I took them away," she added, a mix of worry and sadness in her tone.

Like Blue misses her momma, Autumn thought with a painful tug at her heart. She wanted to reach out and pull her niece into her arms in a comforting hug, but held back giving Tucker a chance to respond. To show he wasn't prepared to deal with the fragile emotions of the young daughter who had been thrust unexpectedly into his life.

"I would never take you away from your aunt Autumn," Tucker said as he started back along the trail, Blue firmly attached to his side. "She's a very important part of your life, and when you come to live with me we'll be sure to visit her often. And, of course, she'll always be welcome here."

He thought Blue was referring to her? She considered correcting his misconception, informing him that it was the loss of her mother that had stirred her niece's concern for the rock's "family," but Blue's next comment as she and her daddy crested the hill had the words faltering at the tip of her tongue.

"Could Aunt Autumn come live here with us, too? So she wouldn't miss me."

Tucker's response was lost to Autumn as he and Blue disappeared over the other side of the hill. Not that she needed to hear the words being spoken to know he'd had to explain to his daughter that her aunt's joining them at the ranch wasn't a possibility. She only prayed he'd done so with soothing words, reassuring her niece that Autumn would still be a very active part of her life if Blue ended up living with him. And Autumn was determined to cling to that *if*, because she wasn't anywhere close to being emotionally prepared to let her niece go. There was still a chance Blue wouldn't want to come to live there with her daddy on his ranch filled with horses. If that were the case, Autumn would, without a moment's hesitation, do everything in her power to keep custody of her.

As she crested the hill behind them, Autumn discovered not a sloping descent, but a slight grassy grade that spilled out onto an expanse of land dotted with flowering bushes. Tucker stood a few feet away with Blue by his side, shrieking in delight as she watched a cloud of brightly colored butterflies hovering above the clusters of yellow flowers that were abloom atop the leafy green bushes.

Autumn gasped as she took in the sight before her.

Never in her life had she seen so many butterflies gathered in one place. Breathtaking didn't even come close to describing the beauty God bestowed before her at that moment.

Tucker glanced back over his broad shoulder. "Worth the climb?"

She moved to stand beside them, her gaze fixed on the fluttering of colorful wings in front of her. "Worth the climb."

They stood in silence for a moment longer before Tucker looked her way. "Last evening when you said you weren't surprised Summer hadn't told me about you, why is that?"

Her lips pressed together for a moment before replying, "Summer and I were twins, but we were two very different people. I secretly envied my sister's ability not to take life so seriously. I always felt the need to shoulder everyone else's problems. But it seems my sister harbored some feelings of jealousy toward me as well, resenting the way people would turn to me when they needed something, especially our grandma, who Summer felt loved me more."

"Did she?" he asked, his tone casting no judgment.

"No," she answered. "Our grandma loved us both the same. I just happened to be the one who was good at caring for sick people, or handling situations that might arise." Eyes tearing up, she said, "Summer only opened up to me about the resentment she felt toward me when her condition worsened. She wanted me to know how grateful she was for the time we had spent together these past few years raising Blue. She was right. It allowed us to reconnect as sisters and friends."

"I'm glad the two of you were able to strengthen your relationship."

"Me, too." So very glad.

Tucker's gaze trailed after his daughter. "How long will you and Blue be staying in Bent Creek?"

She watched her niece, who was now standing amid the gathering of colorful butterflies, and felt an unexpected pang of loss. She hadn't lost Blue to Tucker. And maybe she never would if the Lord answered her prayers. "I've cleared a month from my work schedule to bring Blue out here to meet you and, if your schedule permitted, get to know you better," she told him. "If we end up staying that long, we might have to shop for some additional clothes to wear." It was important that she spend the time to really get a feel for the kind of man Tucker Wade was beyond the research and newspaper clippings her sister had on him. "But I'm not promising we'll be here for the full month. Too many factors come into play." Like his not being the man her sister thought him to be. She needed to know that Summer's faith in Tucker, a man she had chosen to walk out on, was well and truly deserved.

He gave a nod. "Understandable. Then we'll take it day by day. I'm just grateful for the opportunity to get to know my daughter while you and I sort things out."

She didn't want to be there "sorting" things out. If it were up to her, she'd be on her way back to Cheyenne that very moment. But her sister had wanted this, with her dying breath she had wanted this, and so far Tucker Wade was turning out to be a very likable man. One who appeared to be truly eager to spend some real heartfelt time with the daughter he'd never known existed.

"You don't have to worry about Blue and I imposing on you any more than we already have," Autumn said. "I've made a few calls and there are a couple of bed-and-breakfasts nearby that are able to accommodate us during our stay." She hadn't made any concrete reservations before setting out for Bent Creek, unsure of how things would go once they'd gotten there. Tucker could have easily rejected the idea of being a father, even argued that he wasn't Blue's daddy, but he hadn't. He'd taken one look at his baby girl and he'd known.

"Your being here isn't an imposition," he said, keeping his voice low.

She looked up at him, arching a skeptical brow. "You've slept in the barn for two nights now." Guilt gnawed at her for putting him out of his own house, even if she hadn't been the one to suggest it.

"Like I told you yesterday morning, it wasn't the first time."

She tilted her head. "So it's customary to move to the barn when guests arrive here in Wyoming?"

"Not exactly," he answered with a grin. "I'm just saying that when my brothers and I were boys we'd sleep in the barn some nights. There and in the pasture under the stars."

"But you're not a boy any longer," she pointed out. "You're a full-grown man."

"Can't argue that," he teased.

"Tucker," she said in exasperation.

He tempered his smile, his expression turning more serious. "If sleeping in the barn means I'll have my daughter close by, then I'm more than willing to do so. I want you and Blue to feel comfortable. Say you'll stay on here at the ranch."

"Tucker…"

"Please."

She appreciated his giving up his own comfort for theirs, but if they stayed on she wouldn't spend her days feeling guilty for chasing him out of his own house. "I won't have you sleeping in the barn on our account," she said firmly. "If we decide to accept your hospitality for our stay here, you have to promise me you'll sleep in your own bed and not out in the barn."

"I promise."

"Then we'll stay."

He smiled down at her. "Just so you know, I would've agreed to sleep in a briar patch if that's what it took."

Before she could reply, Blue exclaimed excitedly, "Now I know why the rocks wanna come up here. They would get to live with butterflies!"

Autumn felt the confidence she'd had in Blue's wanting to remain with her in Cheyenne slipping just a notch. But her niece wouldn't be living up on a hill surrounded by butterflies. She'd be living on a ranch with strangers, relatives or not, surrounded by horses which she was now painfully leery of.

Blue giggled, drawing Autumn's attention her way. A blue-and-green butterfly had come to rest on her niece's tiny shoulder. Blue's gaze shot up to Tucker as it fluttered away. "He thought I was a flower," she exclaimed.

"Because you are," he replied. "Bluebells are among the prettiest of all flowers."

Her niece's face lit up at her daddy's compliment.

Autumn fought to suppress a groan. It was no wonder her sister had been so taken with this man and his sweet words. How was she supposed to compete with uncles and grandparents, blue skies filled with rainbow-colored butterflies and a daddy who was such a smooth-talking cowboy he always seemed to know just the right thing to say?

Chapter Four

Tucker pulled up to his house, relief sweeping over him when he saw Autumn Myers's sporty little car still parked in his drive. While he had set out early that morning to tend to ranching duties, just as he had for the past several days, it was the first time he'd felt a nagging sense of unease about leaving. His gut told him that Autumn, who seemed to have enjoyed their outing to see the butterflies three days earlier, had even agreed to stay on at the ranch for an undetermined amount of time, was having second thoughts about her decision to remain in Bent Creek.

It hadn't been anything she'd said. It was more in her actions. After their playful hike up the hill in search of some blooming rabbitbrush and the butterflies he knew would be hovering around it, Autumn had been less free with her smiles when it came to him. As if she had decided to put up some sort of emotional wall between them. He supposed he couldn't really blame her. In her eyes, he was the enemy. The person who could take away the very thing she loved most. And there was nothing he could say that would ease her worry, because Blue was his daughter. She belonged with him. That didn't mean he wanted to push her from Blue's life. Far from. Family was, and had always been, important to him and Autumn was all that remained of Blue's mother's side.

That morning, before he'd headed to the main barn, which sat on his parents' property a few miles down the road, Autumn had been unusually quiet. Not that his daughter's excited ramblings over the stray kitten that had shown up the day before, no doubt Garrett's doing, had left much room for anyone else to speak. More concerning, however, was Autumn's avoidance of any sort of eye contact with him during breakfast that morning.

So, as he'd gone about his ranch work that day, his thoughts had been centered largely on Autumn, wondering if she would just up and leave without a word like her sister had. It was that worry that had Tucker sending a fair share of prayers up to the Lord that day. Whether it had been divine intervention in answer to those prayers, or simply Autumn's decision to remain, his daughter and her aunt were still there.

Tucker didn't think he could bear having his daughter brought into his life only to have her taken away from him again. He didn't even know how to contact them if they had been gone. All he knew was that they lived in Cheyenne, a city with a population somewhere around sixty thousand.

Shutting off the engine, he stepped from the truck and started for the house. Three strides in, the front door opened, followed by the screen door as his daughter shot outside to greet him. "Daddy!"

Tucker's heart squeezed at the exuberant greeting. The sight of his baby girl awaiting him at the edge of the porch, a blanketed bundle in her arms, had a grin spreading across his face. He'd never given much thought to having children, not with his still being legally wed to Summer, and he'd be the first to admit that suddenly finding out he was somebody's father scared the daylights out of him, but he couldn't thank the Lord enough for this precious gift He had bestowed upon him.

Tucker picked up his pace as he cut across the yard. "Did you grow taller since I left to check on the horses this morning?"

His daughter giggled and shook her head, causing the mass of chestnut curls pulled up into a ponytail at the back of her head to swing to and fro. "Nope."

"You sure?" he teased as he reached the porch where Blue stood waiting at the top of the steps. "You look taller."

"That's 'cause I'm standing up here and you're down there."

He couldn't help but feel a surge of pride at her response. His baby girl was a bright little thing. "Ah, that must be it," he replied with a chuckle as he started up the few stairs.

As soon as he stepped up onto the porch itself, Blue set the bundle in her arms down on the floor beside her and then turned to wrap her tiny arms around his legs in an affectionate hug. "I missed you."

There was no stopping the moisture that gathered in his eyes as he stood there, soaking up the love of his baby girl. A pure, trusting love that took time to grow between adults, but seemed to come so easily for children.

"I missed you, too," Tucker managed past the knot in his throat. He glanced down past his daughter to the tiny head that had just popped out from beneath the covering of the old lap blanket. "Well, look who's still here."

"Bitty was taking a nap," his daughter announced with a smile.

"Bitty, huh?" Tucker returned her smile, making a mental note to thank his brother for the tiny calico kitten he'd left on the front doorstep for Blue in a small wooden crate. Not that anyone had seen Garrett dropping the kitten off, but Tucker had seen that very same crate in his brother's office two weeks past.

The sleepy-eyed calico stepped free of its covering and gave a long, yawning stretch.

His daughter nodded. "I called her that 'cause she's itty-bitty."

"That she is," Tucker agreed, glancing down to watch as the kitten wound its way around his leg as if in greeting and then wandered off across the porch.

"Where's she going?" Blue said in a panic as she watched her kitten go.

"I'm sure Bitty's hungry after her nap," he told her. "She's probably off to hunt for some field mice. She'll be back."

The screen door creaked open behind them, drawing both of their gazes away from the departing kitten.

Autumn stepped out to join them on the porch, that smile he'd been wishing for taking him by surprise as it moved across her face. "Hello," she greeted.

"Hello," he replied, thinking that this was what his life could have been like if Summer hadn't taken it all away. A family there to welcome him home when his work was done each day—affectionate little kitten included. But that wasn't his life. And Autumn wasn't his wife. In fact, she was turning out to be nothing at all like her sister had been. He couldn't help but wonder what his marriage might have been like if Summer had been a little more like her steadfast, loving twin.

"You're early," she said a little anxiously.

Tucker nodded. He had cut his day a little short because of fears that now seemed to have been unfounded. Autumn hadn't run off like Summer had. But placing his trust in another woman didn't come easy for him. His wife had seen to that. "Ranchers don't keep the usual business hours."

"I should've known that," she said almost apologetically.

"I wouldn't expect you to." He noted that she hadn't taken the time to put on her jacket. Instead, she stood, arms folded as she braced against the gentle bite of the fall air. A dish towel dangled from one of the hands curled about the sleeves of her blouse.

Following the line of his gaze, she said, "I was doing up some dishes when I heard Blue go outside."

Blue looked up at her. "I saw Daddy's truck out the window."

Noting that his daughter wasn't wearing a jacket either, he mentally scolded himself for not noticing sooner. Scooping Blue up, he said, "Let's get the two of you back in the house. The air's a little brisk outside today."

Autumn nodded in agreement and then turned to hold the door open as Tucker carried his daughter inside.

Once there, he lowered Blue to her feet and turned to Autumn. "I wasn't so sure you'd be here when I got home today. And I want you to know that if I've done or said anything to make you feel even the least bit uncomfortable, I'm sorry."

She shook her head. "You haven't done anything. If I'm a little out of sorts, it's because of everything going on in my life right now. At times, it can be overwhelming."

"Understandable. Know that I appreciate your choosing to see this through."

"I'm doing this for Blue. She deserves to have the chance to get to know her daddy," she said, glancing down at her niece.

He looked to Blue and smiled. "Her daddy is so happy to have her here."

Blue returned his smile. "Aunt Autumn said we get to keep living with you!"

Autumn shook her head. "Not live with, sweetie. We're only visiting with your daddy for a spell." She looked up at Tucker, meeting his gaze. "I—" The sound of approaching vehicles outside drew her gaze toward the narrow windowpanes that lined the front door.

Tucker looked past her and then rolled his eyes with a groan. "I told them they're becoming pests."

"Told who?" Autumn asked.

"My brothers," he grumbled.

"My uncles!" Blue exclaimed as she raced over to one of the windows to peer out.

"I'll take care of this," Tucker said as he moved toward the door.

"Where are you going?" Autumn asked as she started after him.

"To send them on their way."

"Why do they gotta leave?" Blue whined.

He stopped, turning to his daughter. "Because they've dropped by nearly every day since you've been here. I told them both that they need to give the two of you some breathing room."

"I don't need room," Blue said. "See." She drew in a deep breath and then let it out.

"Tucker," Autumn said, reaching out to place a staying hand on his arm. "I'd like for you to invite them to stay for supper."

"Yay!" Blue exclaimed, clapping her hands excitedly.

Tucker searched her face. "You sure about that?" He didn't want her to feel more overwhelmed than she already was, which his brothers in their eagerness to interact with their niece might have a tendency to do.

She smiled. "I'm sure. Besides, it'll give me a chance to see how they are with Blue for a longer period of time than the brief visits they've made here this week."

That was precisely what he was afraid of. Dinner might not work out in his favor if that were the case. Jackson and Garrett, whose hearts were in the right place, were every bit as clueless as he was when it came to children. Put the three of them together and Autumn was bound to focus on all the reasons not to leave Blue in their care instead of the most important reason—they were family. And family stayed together. They loved each other unconditionally, had each other's back and held strong in their faith.

"I'll extend the invite," he said, praying they wouldn't send Autumn running for the hills with his daughter in tow. "Dinner won't take long to put together. I picked up a couple of boxes of spaghetti last time I was at the grocery store. Should be enough to feed all of us, and I can whip it up pretty quick."

"That won't be necessary," Autumn told him. "I've already prepared this evening's supper. I'll just go preheat the oven and stick it in to warm for a spell."

His brows shot up. "You did?"

"I helped her," Blue said with a bright smile. "It's a surprise. Are you surprised?"

Looking down into Autumn's pretty ice-blue eyes, he said, "Very."

"It's not spaghetti," she said, almost anxiously, "but there should be more than enough to feed two additional dinner guests."

Whatever it was, he appreciated her having gone to the trouble of making dinner. He'd been doing all the cooking that week. And what man didn't appreciate coming home to a home-cooked meal? "I'm sure whatever you came up with will be more than fine," he told her. "But you didn't have to make anything. You're my guest. I should be cooking for you."

"Blue and I thought it was time we made dinner for you."

His daughter nodded in agreement.

Autumn's gaze lifted and there was no missing the hint of concern in those thickly-lashed blue eyes of hers. "I hope you don't mind."

"Mind?" he said, shaking his head. "Not at all. It's nice coming home to find I've had a surprise dinner planned for me." It was a small taste of the kind of life he might have had. But warm welcomes home and special dinners had been denied him. First by Summer, and then by his own determination never to risk his heart again. He'd remained married when he could have tracked Summer down to end things legally. It guaranteed that he couldn't—wouldn't—make the same mistake twice. If only the past few days hadn't shown him what that decision had cost him.

Tucker cleared his throat and looked back toward the door. "I guess I'll go extend that invite." Not that his brothers wouldn't have made their way to the house without one. Stepping outside gave him the chance to sort through his rambling thoughts and, at the same time, distance himself from the woman responsible for them being that way.

"Thank you for inviting us to dinner," Garrett said to Autumn as he settled into the chair next to Tucker's. His warm, lone-dimpled grin was the carbon copy of not only his brothers', but his niece's, as well.

Jackson nodded. "Yes, thank you. We only meant to stop by for a visit." He looked to Tucker. "Against my brother's orders I might add."

She couldn't help but smile at the glower Tucker was shooting them both. "I heard. However, I'm glad you did. It'll give me a chance to see how you all interact as a family."

"Probably not the best month to look for us to be overly loving to each other," Jackson muttered as he stabbed a forkful of chicken from the oval-shaped dish in the center of the table and dropped it onto his plate.

Autumn looked his way. "Excuse me?"

"It's October," Garrett added, as if that explained everything.

"We're coming off the back end of rodeo season," Tucker explained. "That means after putting in thousands of miles together while taking our stock to the dozens of rodeos we were contracted for, we tend to feel a little less warm and fuzzy toward each other."

"Fuzzy?" Blue piped in. "Like my teddy bear?"

Garrett chuckled. "Not quite, little darlin'. What your daddy's saying is that we tend to need a little breathing room from each other right after rodeo season ends."

"To keep us from wanting to strangle each other," Jackson added.

Blue's eyes widened with worry.

"Wrangle," Tucker blurted out as he cast a chastising glance in his brother's direction. "Your uncle meant to say to keep us from wanting to wrangle each other."

"What's wrangle?" she asked.

"That means to argue over something," Autumn answered for them as the three men sat exchanging troubled glances, no doubt realizing the current flow of their dinnertime discussion wasn't in their best interest when it came to convincing Autumn her niece would be in good hands with them. Then she turned to Tucker, focusing on something else that had been said. "Thousands of miles?"

He winced, looking as if he wanted to kick himself. "It's not as bad as it sounds. Rodeo season is only a few months long and for smaller events usually only two of us go."

She nodded, her gaze dropping to Blue. "Sounds very time-consuming."

"It can be," he answered honestly. "But I'm willing to change up my schedule to accommodate my daughter's needs. And my parents will be more than willing to help out whenever necessary."

"I see," she said stiffly. "I guess that means they took the news of their having a granddaughter well, then?" Autumn could only imagine what a shock such a revelation must have been for them.

Anxious glances were exchanged among the three men.

Seeing the men's sudden unease, she looked to Tucker, pinning him with her gaze. "Your parents still don't know?"

His frown returned. "Not yet. But not because I'm worried about how they'll react to hearing they have a granddaughter. I just wanted a few days to let all of this settle in before calling them."

"It's been a few days," she responded flatly, disappointed that he felt the need to keep news of his having a daughter from the very people who brought him into this world.

"What my little brother's not saying," Garrett cut in, "is that he knows Mom and Dad will pack up and rush back to Bent Creek the moment they find out about Blue."

"And that would be a bad thing why?" she asked.

"Because they've been talking about taking this trip to Jackson Hole for as long as any of us can remember," Jackson said. "When Mom was hospitalized with pneumonia this past spring, Dad told her she had to get better because he was buying an RV and taking her on that trip she'd been longing for."

So Tucker wasn't hiding the fact of Blue's existence out of any sort of shame or embarrassment—he was doing so out of consideration for his parents' long-awaited trip. She found herself warming up to this kind-hearted cowboy with each passing day.

Maybe if Tucker had known about the baby her sister had been carrying at the time, things might have turned out differently for them all. He might have chosen to settle down in one place. Made something of their hasty marriage. But he hadn't known. Her sister's decision had not only deprived the man of his daughter, it had deprived Blue of the chance to know her father and all the family that came with him.

"I'm hungry," Blue said, squirming restlessly in her chair.

"You and me both," Tucker said with a smile directed

specifically at his little girl. "We should eat before this meal your aunt Autumn made us gets cold."

"Can I say the prayer?" her niece asked, casting a pleading glance in Autumn's direction.

"That would be nice," Autumn told her. "Now close your eyes and bow your head."

Blue did just that and began in her soft little voice, "Thank You, Lord, for this meal we're gonna eat. And for my new daddy. Amen."

Her niece's words had a happy smile stretching wide across Tucker's handsome face.

"Oh, and thank You for my uncles, too," Blue added, folding her hands together and squeezing her eyes shut once more. "They're really tall. And for Aunt Autumn. She sells houses. And for all the pretty butterflies that live over the hill. And—"

"Sweetie," Autumn said, gently cutting her off, "why don't we finish thanking the Lord for all of the blessings he's bestowed upon us when we go to bed tonight?" There was no telling how many more things Blue had yet to be grateful for. Autumn fought to suppress the pinch of hurt she felt while Blue was giving her thanks. She reckoned she should be grateful her niece had placed her above the butterflies, but there was a time not too long ago—six days ago to be exact—that she was at the top of Blue's prayer list. Now Tucker seemed to be the center of her niece's world and Autumn knew she'd be lying to herself if she didn't say that it hurt just a little. "Your daddy and your uncles have to be very hungry after working on the ranch all day."

"But I didn't get to thank God for the chicken we picked up at the store 'cause you burned—"

"Amen," Autumn blurted out, cutting her niece off.

"Everyone dig in." Cheeks warming, she leaned over to tuck a dinner napkin down into the front of Blue's shirt. When she turned back to reach for her own napkin to place it on her lap, she found three big, strong cowboys grinning at her. Her face warmed even more.

"Something you're not telling us?" Tucker asked, dark brows raised in question.

She groaned, knowing if she didn't fess up, Blue would do it for her. "I might have accidentally allowed the water to boil away while cooking that spaghetti you mentioned having just bought at the store."

The corner of Tucker's mouth twitched. "You burned spaghetti?"

Could this moment get any more embarrassing? The last thing she needed was for Tucker Wade to tally up reasons for her not to be the best choice when it came to raising Blue. Reason number one—her poor cooking skills. There was no getting around that fact. Showing houses and nursing the elderly was her specialty. Summer had been the one more at home with horses and in the kitchen.

Ignoring Tucker's teasing grin, Autumn said, "You told us to help ourselves to anything we wanted from the kitchen while you were away. Blue came across the spaghetti in the pantry while we were fixing our lunch. She asked if we could surprise you with it for dinner. I thought it was the least we could do, considering your opening your home to us during our stay here. And spaghetti isn't all that hard to make as long as you don't let the water boil away."

"'Cause the noodles can catch fire," Blue stated as she dipped her spoon into the small mound of mashed potatoes on her plate. "That's why we had to go to the store to shop for dinner."

The men's dimples disappeared as their mouths dropped open.

"Fire?" Tucker choked out.

"The smoke was stinky," Blue added, crinkling her nose.

"There were no actual flames," Autumn said in her own defense. "Just a little smoke."

"Not as much as that time we made brownies," her niece agreed. "And not as stinky as when you burned my hot chocolate." Blue's expression changed, her gaze dropping to the plate in front of her. "Momma made the best hot chocolate."

The humor faded from Tucker's eyes at the mention of Summer, not that Autumn could blame him. Because of her sister, Blue had no fond memories of her daddy as she was growing up.

"Your grandma Wade's hot chocolate is pretty good, too," Tucker told Blue. "She'll have to make you some when she gets home."

Blue gave a small nod, but the sadness still filled her face.

Autumn hated feeling as though she had failed her niece. If only Summer were still with them. Life could go back to the way it had been when they'd all been happy. Would her sister have ever told her the truth about Tucker? Or would she have gone on letting Autumn believe the worst about Blue's daddy?

She glanced over to find Tucker watching her and shrugged apologetically. "Except for baking an occasional berry pie, cooking has never been my forte." And she was only good at that because she used to bake a berry pie every year for the annual pie Bake-Off back home in Braxton.

"I can't even make a pie," Tucker admitted. "So you're one up on me."

Garrett nodded. "I'd take chicken over spaghetti any day, so I guess that makes me glad you let the water boil away."

"This meal looks a lot more appetizing than some of the meals Tucker has served us in the past," Jackson muttered. "Although I'll admit his cooking has improved greatly over the years."

She gave them a grateful smile, but all she could focus on was the fact that Tucker Wade could cook. Another point in his favor.

"Nothing wrong with store-bought chicken," Jackson said as he stuffed a forkful of the rotisserie-baked chicken into his mouth.

They were being so kind, despite the resentment they had to feel, having Blue kept from them for so long. Autumn felt the sting of tears and knew she was on the verge of an emotional breakdown. "Please excuse me," she said, pushing away from the table. As she stood, all three men did so, as well. Their mannerly gesture had her stifling a sob.

"Aunt Autumn?" The concern in Blue's voice held Autumn in place for a long moment, but her niece would be more worried if her aunt were to break down right in the middle of dinner.

"It's okay, sweetie," she said, her voice breaking slightly. She prayed the Lord would grant her the strength to hold it together until she could make her way out of the room. "There's something Aunt Autumn needs to do before I eat. But you can go ahead and start without me. I won't be long." That said, she turned and hurried from the kitchen.

"Autumn?" Tucker called after her.

She didn't stop. Couldn't stop. Not when it felt like the weight of the world was pressing down on her.

Booted footsteps followed her out onto the front porch and down the steps into the front yard.

"Autumn, please," Tucker said. "Tell me what's wrong."

She kept on walking, tears sliding down her cheeks. "I'm okay," she called back over her shoulder. "Please go back inside and enjoy your dinner."

Instead of doing as she asked, he lengthened his stride, easily catching up to her. "You're crying," he said in surprise. "If this is about the spaghetti…"

"It's not," she said, fighting to hold back the tears. "Well, maybe it is a little."

"If my teasing you about it upset you, I apologize," he said, sounding truly remorseful. "I suppose I'm used to having my brothers around. We're always trying to get each other's goat."

"Summer did most of the cooking," she said, her bottom lip quivering. "But it's not just about my below-par cooking skills. Or your finding humor in my burning the spaghetti. It's wanting it so very badly for this to be just some awful nightmare I'm gonna wake up from. Not so much you or your brothers, but the losing my sister part. Very possibly my niece, as well," she added with a hiccupping sob. "Blue is the only family I have left and, while I'm trying to leave it in the Lord's hands, I'm terrified my prayers won't be answered." Just as they hadn't been when she'd prayed to the Lord not to take her sister from them.

"Autumn," he said with an empathetic sigh. Drawing her into his comforting embrace, he rested his chin atop her head as her silent sobs made her shoulders tremble. "I can't even begin to imagine what you've had to go through, but I thank the Lord Blue had you in her life when Summer passed."

For the first time since her sister died, Autumn was the one being comforted. All her efforts and emotional energy following Summer's accident had gone toward consoling Blue. She'd held back her grief, not wanting to cause her niece any more sadness than she was already feeling after losing her mother. Suddenly that grief was spilling out and she was helpless to stop it.

Tucker held her, soothing her with words of comfort and faith as the tears came full force, her sobs no longer silent. When the storm of emotions finally subsided, Autumn lifted her head from Tucker's tear-dampened shirtfront and pushed away. "I'm sorry. I don't know where that came from." She couldn't even bring herself to look him in the eye after such an emotional outburst.

"Grief has no time limit," he said softly, "stirring up when you least expect it. I know because I still have moments when the loss of my sister hits me."

Autumn lifted her gaze to his. "You lost a sister? Summer never said anything."

"That's because she didn't know about her," he said solemnly. "Mari's death is something I avoid talking about, even with my family."

Yet, he was sharing his loss with her? She couldn't help but be touched by it. "How old was your sister when you lost her?"

"Six."

Dear Lord, she was practically a baby. "What happened?" As soon as the question was out, Autumn shook her head. "You don't have to answer that."

"Meningitis," he answered anyway. "She'd had a really bad ear infection that worked its way into her bloodstream. By the time the doctors figured out that it was something more serious and began treatment, Mari had taken a turn for the worse. The Lord called her home that same night."

She had come there with so many preconceived notions about Tucker Wade that were nowhere close to the man she was coming to know. And now they shared another bond, beyond that of her niece. They had both experienced the pain of losing a sibling. A sister.

She wiped at the dampness left behind on her cheeks by her tears. "Thank you for opening up to me about Mari." Especially after admitting that he never spoke of her with anyone, even Summer.

He shrugged as if what he'd just done hadn't been a huge emotional undertaking for him. "I didn't want you to think you were alone when it came to losing a sister. I've always had my brothers to lean on."

"That was very kind of you." She lifted her gaze to look up at him, tears once again filling her eyes. "More kindness than I deserve." Tucker opened his mouth, no doubt to contradict her statement, but Autumn didn't give him the chance to. She owed him the truth. "It wasn't my choice to bring Blue here."

He nodded. "And I appreciate your respecting your sister's last request."

"It was the right thing to do. But I came here already resenting you and the unwanted changes you might bring about in my life," she admitted. "I came here determined to uncover all of your faults and failings, so I could take

Blue home for good. But you're nothing like the man in my imaginings. You're kind and compassionate. You seem to have a natural inclination to know all the right things to say and do when it comes to Blue. And you can cook," she added with a sniffle. "How am I supposed to compete against someone who has no flaws?"

"No flaws?" He snorted. "Sweetheart, I'm the furthest thing from perfect there is. I procrastinate when it comes to cleaning out the fridge, or going grocery shopping. I don't always take time to shave," he said, scrubbing a hand over his lightly stubbled chin. "And I always forget to put the lid back on the toothpaste. Should I go on?"

His words brought a smile to her face. "I'll be sure to make note of those particular flaws when making my final decision."

"You know this doesn't have to be a 'someone wins and someone loses' situation. We can work this out together."

"Tucker, it's not that simple," Autumn replied, her expression growing serious once more.

"Life never is," he said. "But you learn to work around it."

"Like it or not, someone is gonna lose in this situation." She just prayed that someone wouldn't end up being her niece.

He frowned. "I'll be the first to admit I don't have all the answers right now, but I do know one thing. I want my daughter to be happy. Placing her in the middle of a lengthy custody battle isn't going to make that happen, so I intend to do a lot of praying to the Lord for guidance as we work through this situation."

Tucker had been denied his only child. He could easily have turned his bitterness for what her sister had done to him on her and gone straight to his attorney to fight for custody of Blue, which he had every right to. But he had put his daughter's emotional well-being first and was taking the time to get to know her, allowing her time to get to know him, as well.

"Dragging my niece through a court battle is something I'd prefer to avoid as well, if at all possible."

"Then we will," Tucker said assuredly. He cast a quick glance over his shoulder and then back to Autumn. "Look, this probably isn't the best time for us to have this conversation. Blue's bound to start wondering where we've run off to. Why don't we head back inside and have some of that chicken dinner you put together for us?"

"Maybe you should go on in and make excuses for me. My eyes must look awful after crying the way I did."

"Your eyes are as pretty as ever," he said and then cleared his throat as if immediately regretting his words. "I mean they're not the least bit swollen. Come back in and join us. Later, we both can begin mulling over ways to make this situation work for all involved. That is," he added with a slight grin, "if my flaws don't prove to be far too numerous."

With a nod, she walked with him back to the house, a smile pulling at her lips. Tucker Wade thought her eyes were pretty. "Just see that they don't, Mr. Wade. I would hate to add any more flaws to the list I'm mentally compiling to the ones you've already given me."

He let out a husky chuckle. "Appears I'm my own worst enemy."

"Tell you what," she said as they made their way up onto the porch. "You forget about my burning the spaghetti and I'll cross all previously mentioned flaws off of my list."

He glanced her way as he reached for the screen door, and a wide smile spread across his tanned face, the sight of which made her heart skip a beat. "Spaghetti? What spaghetti?"

Chapter Five

Movement in the kitchen entryway had Tucker glancing up from the cup of coffee he was finishing off before heading out to the main barn. For a moment, it was Summer he saw standing there, the thought of which had Tucker's jaw clenching even though he knew that it couldn't be his wife.

Autumn's shoulder-length hair, at least where the cut fell in the front, was slightly mussed, as if she'd taken a walk outside where a slight breeze filled the cool, crisp morning air. Instead of the more polished, professional dress style he'd seen her wear since coming to the ranch, she was dressed in an oversized loose-fitting sweatshirt and a pair of black leggings, reminding him more of her sister in her casual attire.

But this wasn't Summer. Acknowledging that, he managed a smile. "Morning."

"Morning," Autumn replied as she moved into the room.

Pushing away from the table, Tucker stood. "I hope I didn't wake you."

She shook her head. "You didn't. I've been up for a

while, going through work emails. I heard you moving about the kitchen. Do you have a moment to talk? There's something I really needed to say to you."

Tucker's gut tightened. Was this the day she had made the decision to head back to Cheyenne with his daughter? Nine days was not nearly enough time to sway Autumn over. And the last thing he wanted to do was to hurt her any more than she was already hurting. He'd seen the emotional pain she tried so hard to hide.

"I'll make time," he said as he stepped around the table to slide a chair out for her. "Can I get you something? A cup of coffee? A glass of orange juice?"

"No, thank you," she replied as she took the offered seat with a grateful smile. "We really haven't had any time alone to speak," she began. "You've either been working the ranch, or others have been around. Your brothers. Blue."

He nodded in understanding. Though he'd cut back on the hours he spent working during her and Blue's stay there, Autumn was correct about their really having no time for any private conversation between the two of them. Blue rarely left his side when he returned home, except for when he went out to the barn. And Garrett and Jackson had been by several times that past week to visit. His brothers had even hung a wooden swing from one of the trees in the front yard for Blue to play on, which his daughter happily spent hours on.

"You should have said something," he told her as he returned to his seat. "I would've found time for us to talk in private."

"I was gonna last night, but you had plans," she replied. "I'm sorry to have left you and Blue here to entertain yourselves last night, but I had a prior obligation I didn't feel right backing out of."

"Of course not," she said. Yet, Tucker wondered if he shouldn't have called the nursing home to tell them he wouldn't be in while his daughter was visiting. But he'd needed to check in on Old Wylie, and see how he was recovering after his recent struggle with gout. The long-retired rodeo cowboy had no family to look in on him, so Tucker had taken it upon himself to watch out for him. Thankfully, his old friend had appeared to be hale and hearty. Like the Old Wylie who had taught Tucker so much of what he knew about being a professional rodeo rider. And for that Tucker was grateful.

"What was it you wanted to talk about?" Tucker asked, preparing himself for the worst, hoping for the best.

Autumn lowered her gaze to the table. "This has been weighing on my mind since last week, so I figured it was time to get it out in the open."

His heart sank. "Sounds serious."

"Not so much serious as it is embarrassing," she mumbled with a frown, her gaze still downcast.

"Embarrassing?"

Autumn looked up and he immediately noted the hint of color in her cheeks. "I'm referring to my teary out-burst last week. I think I owe you an apology for my behavior that evening, though it's a rather belated one at this point."

Relief swept through him for the umpteenth time since Autumn's arrival. She wasn't there to tell him she and Blue were leaving. The tension in his limbs immediately eased. That past week had been a series of emotional ups and downs for him. At times, tension rode him hard, knowing he had to prove himself not only to Autumn but to his little girl. He couldn't—no, he wouldn't let his daughter down. But there was also that niggling doubt at the back of his mind—what if he failed? Then there were those times when Blue would hug him so lovingly, so acceptingly, or when Autumn would grant him a heartfelt smile, making him feel less like her enemy and more like…well, more at ease, that his confidence in his ability to be Blue's father buoyed.

"You don't have anything to be embarrassed about," he told her. "Or apologize for." He curled his fingers around the ceramic mug on the table in front of him to keep from reaching out to cover her hand with his as he had the sudden urge to. Autumn touched a soft spot inside him. One he hadn't known still existed. His wife's leaving all those years before had hardened his heart where other women were concerned. Not that he couldn't be kind to them, or blame them for what Summer had done. He had just gotten used to being emotionally unavailable. But something had changed after Autumn and his little girl had come into his life.

"I never should have allowed my emotions to spill out the way they did," she said. "That was so unlike me. I'm normally the one responsible for holding things together. Not collapsing into a puddle of uncontrollable tears."

He lifted his gaze to hers. "I get what you're going through. Losing a sibling is probably one of the hardest things a person can go through in their life. At least, you're able to talk about your sister. It's more than I can say for myself, and far more time has gone by since Mari's passing."

"Only with you." Her softly spoken confession drew his attention once more. "You're the only person I've shared my true feelings with. I would never let Blue see me like that, and I don't really have any close friends in Cheyenne to talk to. I spent all of my free time with Summer and Blue."

"Surely you have other family besides Blue down in wherever it was you grew up in Texas that you can turn to when the grief gets overwhelming."

She looked perplexed for a moment before shaking her head. "Braxton. A town similar in size to Bent Creek." Her frown deepened. "Did you and my sister ever really talk before the two of you eloped?"

He sighed. "Probably not as much as we should have. At least, not about the things that one realizes are important as they grow wiser with age. At the time, we were all about competing in the rodeo and the excitement of falling in love. Or what I guess we both thought to be love at the time."

"In my sister's defense, she didn't grow up with parents who were shining examples of true love. Our daddy was never in the picture and Momma didn't like the picture she was in. She preferred travel and adventure to raising kids. We were cared for mostly by our maternal grandma."

Tucker listened intently, taking in all the information his wife had failed to share with him. Had she believed he would have judged her by her parents' past if she'd shared this information with him? Or was it because she longed to leave her past behind her? So many questions he would never have the answers to.

Autumn went on, drawing Tucker back to the conversation. "Summer and I longed for our momma to show us some sort of motherly love, but we learned pretty young that not everyone's cut out to be somebody's parent. So we shut her out of our hearts."

"I didn't know any of this," he admitted with a frown. "But then your sister always steered our conversations away from her life in Texas."

"I'm not surprised. She wanted to get away from the life we had growing up. And when college didn't turn out to be the answer for her, she went back to barrel racing, which allowed her to leave her past behind doing something she had always loved."

"You've made it clear that you aren't close to your mother, but does she know about Summer's passing?"

"I have to reckon she knows," Autumn replied with a sad smile. "She was killed in a whitewater rafting accident the summer before my sister and I started high school. Grandma Myers became our full-time caretaker, raising us alone through those troubling teen years and loving us until she passed away when we were seventeen. Thankfully we were able to avoid being placed into the system. We both had part-time jobs outside of school and were just shy of turning eighteen, so the judge granted us our emancipation."

He couldn't even fathom what it had been like to live the kind of life she and Summer had. Tucker found himself wanting to wrap Autumn in a comforting embrace, just as he had the evening before. Thankfully there was a table between them to hold him in place. But that didn't keep his heart from going out to her. Life hadn't been easy for Autumn or Summer. Not only because of the losses they had suffered, but because of the love they'd been denied by their parents. He sent up a silent prayer of thanks to the Lord for blessing him and his brothers with a tight-knit family whose foundation was built on love and faith.

"I'm sorry," he said, not knowing what else to say.

She met his gaze, her own glistening with unshed tears. "It was a long time ago." Reaching up, she fingered a small gold cross that hung from a delicate gold chain around her neck.

"Your mother's?" he asked, nodding toward the cross.

"My grandma's," she replied. "She used to tell us it was a reminder of her faith. That wearing it close to her heart helped her to stay strong when times were tough." She let her hand fall away. "Summer didn't care for jewelry, so Grandma Myers left it to me in her will."

He had to imagine Autumn had sought comfort from that precious family heirloom quite often since Summer's passing. Grief was a hard road to travel. Even more so when one tried to walk it alone. He knew that firsthand.

"Are you still in contact with friends back in Texas?" he pressed, needing to know she wasn't completely alone. That she still had someone she could turn to.

"Yes. My best friend lives in Braxton," she answered, and relief swept through him. "Hope moved back to town right before I left for Wyoming, but we stay in touch."

"It's good to know you at least have her to call and talk to when you're feeling down." It was long-distance comfort, but it was better than nothing at all.

"Oh, I wouldn't do that to her," Autumn said, shaking her head.

"Excuse me?"

"Hope went through a really rough time emotionally after leaving Braxton. Now that she's home and has finally found real joy in her life—" she paused, a smile returning to her pretty face as she thought about her friend "—having reunited with and finally married her high school sweetheart, the last thing I would wanna do is bring her down with my troubles. Not that Hope doesn't call to check up on me. I make sure to keep things light, and usually manage to redirect the conversation so we end up discussing her and Logan instead."

"Autumn, she's your best friend," he said with a disapproving frown. "I would think she'd want to know when you're feeling down."

"If things become too much to bear, I'll turn to Hope," she assured him. "But I tend to have pretty strong shoulders. Last week being the exception. And I have the Lord to turn to, even if he doesn't answer my every prayer."

He knew without her saying that Autumn was referring to Summer's dying. He and Autumn had more in common than Tucker thought. They both refused to burden others with their emotional hardships, instead suffering the hurt they harbored inside in silence. He had to admit that it had felt surprisingly good to open up to her about the loss of his own sister. Like a piece of his long-withheld grief over the loss of his sister was finally lifted. He could only pray their talk, brief as it may have been, had offered her the same bit of solace.

"Aunt Autumn?"

Her head snapped around at the sound of her name being called out. "I'm in the kitchen with your daddy."

Blue wandered in all sleepy eyed, her red-brown curls hanging limply over her tiny face. "Are we gonna go see the butterflies this morning?"

"Not this morning, sweetie," Autumn replied. "Your daddy has work to do."

His daughter's lower lip pushed outward. She would go visit her butterflies every day if she had her way. They'd already been back to see them several times. Tucker made sure to take a different route across the ranch each time to get to the base of the hill, giving Blue closer glimpses of the broncs from behind the safety of his truck's window. Each time, he noticed her watching the galloping herd with more and more interest.

"While I can't drive you to see the butterflies this morning, I'd like to show you my barn," Tucker said with a smile.

Blue's expression grew uneasy. "Are there horses in there?"

Since they'd arrived, his daughter had steered clear of his barn and his two saddle horses. Other than giving her the opportunity to be close to horses while inside his truck, he hadn't pushed Blue for more. He had, however, done a fair amount of praying that the Lord would help her make peace with her fears, her nightmares included. And seeing as how his daughter hadn't had a single nightmare since coming to Bent Creek, he knew the Lord had been listening.

"I'm pretty sure my saddle horses are waiting outside in their pen for their morning grain. Would you like to help me feed them this morning?"

"Tucker..." Autumn said softly, no doubt trying to remind him of Blue's fear when it came to horses.

He hadn't forgotten, but he also knew that his daughter needed to face her fears or she would never overcome them. His gaze shifted back to Blue. "What do you say, sweetheart? Want to help Daddy feed his horses this morning?"

Blue took a step back, shaking her head. "I don't like horses."

His smile threatened to sag at his daughter's declaration, but he forced it to remain intact. Tucker wanted so badly to make her fears go away, but seeing the wary look that filled Blue's eyes and pinched her features had him second-guessing his efforts to help her.

"If you don't want to," he began, wondering why he'd ever thought suggesting Blue help him feed his horses that morning was a good idea, "then—"

"I have an idea," Autumn said, cutting him off with a cheery smile aimed in his daughter's direction. "We haven't gotten to see inside your daddy's barn yet and I'd really like to. Why don't you and I walk out with him and just watch while he feeds his horses?" Before Blue could turn the suggestion down, or run from the room in a panic, she added, "We can stand on the other side of the fence and watch while his horses eat their breakfast. Just like we used to do with your momma. Then maybe afterward, your daddy will have time to give us a quick tour of his barn."

Just like she had done with her mother, Tucker thought regretfully. If he had known that, he absolutely wouldn't have suggested it. The last thing he wanted to do was stir up painful memories for his daughter. But how was he to avoid it? He had no idea what kind of memories she had since he'd never been a part of them.

Tucker had just opened his mouth to tell his daughter that she didn't have to go with him to the barn when she surprised him by saying, "I like to feed them apples."

His heavy heart lightened at her words. Blue hadn't written horses out of her life completely. There was, much to his relief, a glimmer of hope that his daughter might yet come around. "They love being fed apples," he told her, a smile stretching wide across his face. "In fact, I think I have a small bucket of apples out in the barn. If you like, you can give them each a couple of slices before they eat their breakfast." His gaze shifted to

Autumn. "And it would be a pleasure to show you ladies around the barn afterward. Not that there's much to see."

Blue giggled as she sidled up against her aunt who was still seated at the table. "I'm not a lady."

Tucker raised a brow, fighting to hide his amusement. "You're not?"

Her head of springy curls shook from side to side. "No."

He sat back in his chair and pretended to study her. "Well, I know you're not a cat. You don't have any whiskers."

She giggled harder and then swiveled her flannel-nightgown-covered backside around in demonstration. "No tail, either."

"True," Autumn joined in. "Not even the tiniest little bobtail that I can see."

"A peacock?" he teased.

"Nope," his daughter said with a determined shake of her head. "No feathers."

He sighed as if in exasperation. "Then I give up. What are you?"

She smiled up at him. "Your little girl."

She'd said it with such pride and happiness, Tucker felt an unexpected rush of what had to be love fill him. Clearing his throat to push away the knot of emotion that had gathered there, he said, "That you are."

"If we're gonna go out to the barn with your daddy, then you need to go get dressed," Autumn told Blue. "We can eat breakfast when we get back."

"Okay!" Skipping excitedly, his daughter bounced out of the room.

"You need to dress warm!" Autumn hollered after her as Blue scampered away. Then she looked to Tucker. "I will go offer my assistance, but Blue's taken a mind to dress herself these days." She stood to leave.

Tucker sprang to his feet, as well.

Autumn laughed softly. "You don't have to do that you know."

"Do what?"

"Stand every time I enter or leave a room."

"Can't help it," he said. "It's how my mother raised us. When a lady enters the room, you stand. Same goes when she takes her leave." He reached for his cowboy hat, placing it atop his head.

"If only all mommas could install such manners in their sons," she said with a smile as she walked away.

"I'll wait for you and Blue out on the porch," he called after her. He needed to call Jackson and let him know he was going to be a little late getting to the main barn that morning. And for a very good reason. Blue was going to give his horses a chance. If only he could get Autumn to let down her walls and give *him* a chance. And he wasn't so sure he meant that solely in regard to his daughter.

Autumn handed Blue her jacket and then grabbed her own from the chair by the guest bed. "We'll need these. Fall mornings can be quite chilly." Unlike the weather she'd grown up in down in Texas.

Her niece slipped her coat on and then waited while Autumn bent to zip her snuggly inside it. "Can Bitty go with us?"

Her gaze drifted over to the tiny ball of speckled white fur perched atop the deep-set windowsill looking out. "I think she's content to sit on the windowsill, soaking up the warming rays of the morning sun. You two can play together after we get back and have had our breakfast."

Blue looked disappointed, but only for a moment before her attention was drawn elsewhere. "Can I take my doll?"

Autumn smiled. "If you want."

Blue ran over to grab the well-loved rag doll from the bed. Then she turned back to Autumn. "We're ready."

"Your daddy is waiting for us outside," Autumn told her as she opened the bedroom door and motioned for Blue to lead the way.

Tucker was standing in the front yard, talking on his phone when they stepped out onto the porch. He gave a wave as he hurried to finish his call. A second later, he shoved the cell phone into the front pocket of his jeans and started toward them. "All set?"

"All set," Autumn told him, taking Blue's hand in hers.

"I see you brought a friend," Tucker said to Blue as they headed for the barn. His normally long strides were noticeably shortened, Autumn had to assume, for their benefit. Always considerate.

Blue appeared pleased that her daddy had noticed her prized possession. "Miss Molly," she told him.

Tucker's step faltered at his daughter's pronouncement.

"She named her doll after something her momma used to say," Autumn explained, sensing he may have already known that by his reaction.

"Good golly, Miss Molly," Tucker muttered as if the saying caused him discomfort. And maybe it did. Her sister had hurt him. He had to be sensitive to things that brought back memories of his runaway wife.

"Did Momma say it to you, too?" Blue asked, looking up at him as they crossed the yard.

"Not to me in particular," he answered. "It was something your mother would say when she was frustrated or surprised over something."

A nearby whinny had Blue's head snapping in that direction. As soon as she saw the two horses watching them from beyond the fence, she sidled closer to Autumn, clutching the floppy rag doll to her chest.

Tucker, whose green-eyed gaze was fixed on the pair of horses, was grinning from ear to ear. "Will you look at that?" he said. "They're excited to see you."

Blue eyed them cautiously. "They are?"

He looked down, no doubt seeing the fear on his daughter's face, and his smile deflated like a party balloon that hadn't been knotted well.

"Maybe Molly can help you feed apples to the horses," Autumn suggested, smiling reassuringly when Tucker's grateful gaze lifted to meet hers.

"Does she have to ride them?" Blue replied, biting at her bottom lip.

"Not if she doesn't want to," he said. "To be honest, I'm not sure I'd have a saddle small enough for her to sit on."

"Can she ride with you?" her niece asked as she released her hold on Autumn's hand to reach for Tucker's.

He was winning her niece over, Autumn thought sadly. And she was helping him to succeed. How foolish was she?

"With me?" Tucker replied, his brows lifting in unison as he looked down at his daughter.

Blue nodded. "In case she's scared."

"And that would make her feel safe?" Tucker queried as he studied his little girl.

Her niece whispered something in her baby doll's ear and then looked up at her daddy once more. "She says it would. 'Cause you're big and strong and wouldn't let her fall."

Was Blue still talking about her doll? Or was this conversation more about her niece's wants and fears? Autumn prayed it was the latter. Her niece used to beg her momma to take her for rides on her horse. It was said that time healed all wounds. Maybe, just maybe, this was the case for Blue.

"If it would make her feel safer," Tucker began, "then I would be more than happy to let Miss Molly ride with me anytime she wants to."

Blue brought the rag doll up to her face once more and then lowered her again. "She says she wants to feed them apples first."

He chuckled. "Miss Molly certainly knows her mind. Why don't you run on into the barn and grab a couple of big fat juicy apples from the bucket sitting just inside the door?"

She hesitated, her gaze fixed on the nearby barn where the wide red door stood partially open.

"There aren't any horses inside," Tucker hurried to assure her. Reaching out, he ran a hand down the nose of the horse closest to him. "I only keep these two here at my ranch. The rest of the horses live at the main ranch where the chickens live."

"Where we collected eggs that day," Autumn reminded her, not that it was necessary. Blue's memory was as sharp as a tack.

"Okay," her niece said, her anxiety about venturing into the barn apparently put to rest by her daddy's reassurance. Blue took off in a happy skip across the yard, her doll flopping around at her side as she went.

Autumn stepped up beside him, watching her niece make her way to the barn to fetch the apples. "I never thought I'd hear her asking to ride a horse again, or see her entering a barn for that matter."

Taking his gaze off Blue, he glanced down. "Blue didn't ask to ride."

Autumn looked up at him in confusion. That was certainly what she'd gotten from the conversation.

"Miss Molly did," he said with a warm chuckle.

Laughter escaped her lips. "I suppose she did. And what a visual that brings to mind. A big, strong cowboy riding around on his horse with a tiny, well-loved rag doll held securely in the saddle in front of him."

He shot her a playful grin. "You forgot handsome."

"I figure that goes without saying," she told him, her words promptly followed by a warmth spreading through her cheeks. She wasn't supposed to notice things like that, even if he had prompted it.

Thankfully, Tucker let the comment go, carrying on as if she hadn't just admitted she thought him handsome. "If it comes down to my having to give Miss Molly a ride, my brothers aren't to hear one word about my doing so."

She couldn't resist. "And if they happen to catch wind of it?"

"They'd never let me live it down. Not to mention the hit my rough and tough cowboy reputation would take."

She appreciated the way he turned things around, joking about his own embarrassment to save her from her own discomfort. "No need to worry," she said with a smile. "Your secrets are safe with me."

Those green eyes studied her for a long moment before Tucker replied, the teasing leaving his tone, "As are yours with me."

Blue came racing out from the barn with an apple in one hand and her doll in the other. She handed Tucker the apple. "This is for the brown horse."

"That's Hoss," he told her.

"What's the other horse's name?"

He glanced toward the pen. "That handsome fellow would be Little Joe."

"I'll be back." She took off for the barn again.

"Where are you going?" Autumn called after her.

"Molly and me gotta go get an apple for Little Joe, too," Blue hollered back over her shoulder as she raced away.

"Yes, we mustn't forget Little Joe," Autumn said, looking to Tucker with a grin. "You wouldn't happen to be a fan of old Westerns, would you?"

"You know *Bonanza*?" he said in surprise.

"You sound surprised."

"I might have expected Summer to have known where my horses' names came from, but not you."

She placed a hand on her hip. "And why ever not?"

He looked her over. "Well, because you aren't exactly the type I picture watching old cowboy shows."

"I'll have you know I've watched several seasons of *Bonanza*. All reruns, of course, but I'm very familiar with the Cartwrights," she told him, chin lifted high.

"I'm impressed."

"Summer had a thing for Little Joe," she admitted. "Myself, I was more partial to Daniel Boone."

"Daniel Boone?"

"Gotta love a man confident enough to walk around in a coonskin hat," she said, making him chuckle.

"I have to confess that out of all the tips my brothers gave me over the years on ways to stir a woman's interest, a coonskin hat was not among them."

"Here we go!" Blue exclaimed as she hurried back with the remaining apple, handing it to her daddy.

"Hoss and Little Joe will be so grateful to you for these apples," Autumn told her as she lifted her niece, placing her atop her hip.

"But God made them," Blue said as she held her doll to her.

"Yes, He did, and I am quite sure your daddy's horses are very grateful to the Lord as well for this sweet feast they are about to receive," Autumn told her as Tucker pulled out his pocketknife and cut into one of the apples. "But you're the one who's bringing these gifts from God to Hoss and Little Joe. I think they'll be mighty grateful to you, as well."

"Your aunt Autumn is right," Tucker said. "Feed them apples and they will love you forever."

"But I'm not gonna feed them," Blue said, her gaze shifting to the horses. "Molly is."

He seemed a bit taken back by the confusion, but recovered quickly. "I think Miss Molly might need a little help holding the apple slices," he told her. "They practically weigh more than she does."

Blue dropped her gaze to the ground, biting into her lower lip.

"Sweetie," Autumn said, "if you decide not to feed your daddy's horses the apples, you and Molly can watch while I feed them." Blue had already taken a huge step by even considering just getting close to the awaiting quarter horses, let alone possibly hand-feeding them.

Her niece's green eyes lifted as she looked sheepishly to Tucker.

He gave her a reassuring smile. "It's okay, sweetheart. You can do it another time if you aren't feeling up to it today."

Blue seemed torn by indecision, looking from her daddy to the horses and back. Then she said something to her doll before saying to Autumn, "You and daddy can feed them. Molly and me will watch."

"I'm guessing your aunt would probably prefer to stand with you and Molly and watch while I feed Hoss and Little Joe some apple slices."

"Your guess would be wrong." She could tell Tucker was surprised by her words and decided to let him in on a little secret. "I might look the business professional type most of the time, but I did grow up in Texas with a sister who lived and breathed horses."

"Momma breathed horses?"

Autumn laughed. "No, sweetie. It's a saying that means she loved everything about them."

"Oh," she said.

She returned her attention to Tucker. "I sometimes helped Summer care for her horse when we were in high school, feeding, watering and grooming him, depending on our work schedules. You might even be shocked to learn that I have even ridden a horse before."

Tucker chuckled, shaking his head. "You are just chock-full of surprises, Miss Myers."

"Just goes to prove you can't always judge a book by its cover," she said with a sly smile. "Shall we go feed those poor horses before they whinny themselves hoarse trying to get our attention?"

"Good idea," he said, walking alongside her to the pen. "I apologize for the assumption I made."

"Apology accepted," she said softly. "And it's understandable. While most identical twins tend to share the same likes and dislikes, my sister and I were two very different people."

"You say that like it's a bad thing," he commented. "God might have created the two of you as mirror images of one another, but He also chose to give you each your own special individuality." He glanced her way. "You are who you were meant to be."

She had spent so many years growing up dealing with comments that made her feel like she and Summer had somehow failed God by not being alike in every sense. Maybe the separate paths they had taken in life had been gently guided by the hand of God.

"Watch your step," Tucker warned, drawing Autumn from her thoughts. "The ground's a little uneven around here. Don't need you two taking a tumble."

Heeding his warning, Autumn trod carefully, Blue balanced securely on her hip. When they reached the fence, she lowered her niece to her feet just far enough away from the fence so that the horses couldn't reach her with their investigative sniffs unless Blue was ready for them to.

"Boys," Tucker said, "I've brought these pretty ladies…" He paused, his gaze sliding over to Autumn and Blue before amending his words. "Make that one pretty lady and my beautiful baby girl to see you. I'm expecting you both to be on your best behavior around them."

The horses nickered in response.

Tucker nodded. "Why, yes, they do have a special treat for you."

"We do!" Blue exclaimed, stepping closer. "We brought you apples!"

Tucker looked as pleased as punch with his daughter's sudden change of heart where his horses were concerned. He held up one of the apple slices. "You probably already know that it's best to feed horses smaller pieces of apple to avoid their choking on them. Hoss and Little Joe don't always mind their manners as best they should and would most likely try to swallow their apples whole if given the chance."

Autumn watched as Tucker held out his hand, offering the bit of apple to the larger of the two horses, a beautiful sorrel-colored gelding.

"Here you go, Hoss," he said in a soothing tone as the horse sniffed at the apple, finally helping himself to the crunchy slice.

Little Joe whinnied, attempting to nudge his way in past Hoss.

Tucker chuckled. "Okay, okay, you get one, too."

"Can I feed him?" Blue said unexpectedly, drawing everyone's attention her way.

Face beaming, Tucker said, "Sure you can. Step on over here beside me."

Blue edged her way over to him, her nervous gaze fixed on the two horses.

Autumn's heart was in her throat. This was the closest Blue had gotten to a horse since Summer's accident.

Tucker knelt beside her, placing an apple sliver in her hand. "Now hold your hand out slowly so Little Joe can scent what you are giving him. Keep your hand upturned and fingers laid flat so he can nibble the apple right off your hand."

She sidled up against Tucker as if he would protect her from all the bad in the world. And maybe that was how things would be if he kept proving himself worthy of his daughter. Autumn felt the sting of unshed tears at the backs of her eyes. She wasn't ready to give up her niece to Tucker or anyone. Why couldn't he have been different? Arrogant. Closed off. Caring only for his own happiness. Unwilling to be saddled down with a child. But Tucker was none of those things. He was, from what she had researched and now had had time to see for herself, a really good man.

"That's it," she heard Tucker say. "Just like that."

Pushing her troubled thoughts aside, Autumn watched as her niece fed Little Joe from her upturned palm. *Thank You, Lord.*

Blue giggled and began to squirm. "That tickles."

Tucker's husky chuckle resonated in the early morning air. "He's making sure he gets every single morsel of apple from your hand."

Satisfied he had, Little Joe pulled back, chewing on his special treat.

"I think you've definitely made a friend in Little Joe," she told Blue.

Her niece looked to her daddy, who was still kneeling beside her. "Can I be Hoss's friend, too?"

"You want to give him an apple slice?"

She nodded.

Smiling, he handed her another piece. "Have at it, sweetheart."

"Look at me, Aunt Autumn," Blue exclaimed with

another burst of giggles as Hoss nibbled at the apple chunk in her upturned hand.

"Look at you," Autumn said, her voice catching.

Tucker's gaze shifted to Autumn and his smile widened as he held an apple slice out to her. "Join us?"

It meant a lot that Tucker was trying to include her. Especially because it was such a special moment for Blue who was finally pushing past her fear when it came to horses. Coming forward, Autumn accepted the offered fruit.

"All done," Blue announced with a joyous grin as she stepped back from the fence. She hurried to wipe her damp, horse-kissed hand off on her jeans.

Autumn opened her mouth to tell her not to wipe her messy hands on her clean clothes, but then closed it. She wasn't about to do or say anything that would take away the joy Blue was feeling at that moment.

Tucker stood, scooping Blue up in one strong arm. "It's your aunt Autumn's turn now," he said, turning to face her.

Something told Autumn that he was testing her. Not quite believing that she was as comfortable as she claimed to be around horses.

Little Joe whinnied, urging her on.

"Patience is a virtue," she told the horse who had stretched his neck through the open slats of the fence to reach the treat in her hand. Autumn extended her arm, unfurling her fingers, allowing Little Joe access to what he wanted. "Like that, do you?" she cooed as she reached out with her other hand to stroke the horse's neck.

The gelding nickered softly.

"I think he likes you," Tucker said as he stood beside her, grinning.

She snorted. "Only because I'm feeding him."

"Oh, I don't know," he countered. "I think he'd find you likable with or without food."

Autumn glanced up at Tucker. When her gaze met his, her heart gave an odd little start. "I—" Her response was cut short by Blue's sudden shriek.

Arms flailing, her niece tried to grab for her doll as it was pulled into the pen. "Molly!" she cried out.

Tucker set Blue on her feet and then straightened. "Hoss!" he scolded as he climbed into the pen to retrieve the pilfered rag doll.

"He's eating her!" Blue said with a sob.

It certainly did appear that way, Autumn thought with a frown.

"I won't let him eat Molly," Tucker called back as he attempted to coax the horse to release its newly found treasure.

When it didn't appear that Hoss was in a mood to co-operate, Autumn thought it best to get Blue away from the situation. Reaching for Blue's hand, she said, "Let's go back to the house and see about fixing you some pancakes."

"What about Molly?" Blue whimpered, craning her neck to look behind her as Autumn led her away.

"Your daddy will get her back after Hoss is through playing with her," she replied, trying to sound as if she believed that to be true. "Then he has to get to work. Your uncles are expecting him. Molly will just have to go help with the chores and then your daddy will bring her home when they are all done."

"Okay," Blue said with a disappointed sigh. "Do you think Daddy will give Miss Molly a ride on his horse if he rides it to work today?"

Autumn managed a smile. "You can count on it." After what had just occurred, she had a feeling Tucker would take Miss Molly out for a fancy dinner if the doll requested it. She just prayed her niece's favorite toy hadn't become dinner herself.

Chapter Six

Tucker took a break from the loose fence post he'd been reinforcing to grab a bottle of water from the insulated cooler bag he kept in his truck. Bringing the bottle to his lips, he took several long swallows as he looked out over his handiwork. The repair was taking longer than usual, but then his focus wasn't fully on the task at hand. It was on Blue.

His gaze shifted to the dirty, mangled doll lying atop the passenger seat of his truck. Miss Molly. Tucker's stomach knotted. Twisting the lid back onto the bottle, he shoved it back into the cooler and then reached for the doll. Its yarn hair, or what remained of it after Hoss had chewed on it, was now matted and damp.

He stepped back and held it up, frowning as the sun spotlighted the extent of the damage that had been done to Miss Molly. Not only was this bound to make Blue dislike horses even more, he couldn't help but wonder if she'd blame him for it, as well. After all, Hoss was his horse. And he'd been the one holding Blue, making it easier for the hungry gelding to make a grab for her doll. Hand dropping to his side, he leaned back against his pickup, his gaze drifting toward the herd of broncs that were grazing and frolicking in the distance. At least, they were having fun. They'd earned it. After months of rodeo competition, these finely-honed, well-bred horses had done the Triple W proud, serving up countless award-winning and championship rides. They were not only his and his brothers' livelihood, they were, without a doubt, their pride and joy. The horses were as close to having children as any of the Wade brothers had ever gotten. Until Blue.

Now Tucker was a daddy, one whose baby girl feared these proud and majestic creatures before him. A fear she had bravely tried to get past that morning when she'd volunteered to hand-feed an apple to Little Joe. Then Hoss had to go and snatch Miss Molly right out of his daughter's hand.

Tucker bit back a groan of frustration. How was he supposed to convince Blue to come to live with him at the ranch, a horse ranch, when even her doll didn't appear to be safe from harm's way when it came to his horses?

Tires rumbled across the ground just beyond his truck. Tucker craned his neck to see who it was.

His brother Jackson pulled up next to Tucker's pickup and cut the engine. Then he stepped out and rounded the front of his truck, peeling off his thick leather work gloves as he went. "You planning on doing any work today, or are you just admiring the view?"

Tucker pushed away from his truck, muttering, "I've been working. Trying to, at least."

"Everything okay?" Jackson asked, his tone far less jesting. "I know it's been quite a shock, finding out about…" His words trailed off as his gaze dropped down to Tucker's clenched hand. "Is that a rag doll?"

"Used to be," he muttered, holding the remnants of Miss Molly up for his brother to see.

Jackson arched a brow. "What happened to it?"

He looked down at the limp, nearly headless doll and his gut twisted. "Hoss decided to floss his teeth with Miss Molly's hair."

"Miss Molly?"

"Blue's doll," he grumbled, as if he really needed to clarify that.

Jackson let out a low whistle. "Looks to me like he tried to floss with her entire head."

Tucker shot him a glare. "You're not helping matters." He already knew the doll was ruined. Blue's treasured little doll was now a stump in a dirty, horse-slobbered dress.

"Does Blue know?" his brother asked, concern knitting his brows.

"Not the extent of the damage my horse did," he said. "But she was there when Hoss made off with her doll. Autumn took Blue back to the house, pretty much in tears." He looked to Jackson. "How am I supposed to tell my little girl that her precious rag doll is done for? She's already lost her mother."

Jackson nodded. "That won't do." He stroked his chin in thought, his gaze fixed on the doll. Then his expression eased. "I've got a plan."

"I'm all ears."

"We'll take Miss Molly to Garrett."

Tucker stared at his brother in confusion. "Taking this doll to Garrett is supposed to fix everything?"

"He's a doctor, isn't he?"

"He's a vet," Tucker said in frustration. "Molly isn't a cow ready to calve, or a horse with digestive issues. She's a rag doll." Glancing down, he added disheartened, "Half a rag doll."

Jackson grabbed Miss Molly from Tucker and started back around his truck.

"Where are you going?" Tucker called after him.

"Get in," his brother said. "We're going into town to buy a mop before we go hunt Garrett down."

"A mop?" *Had his brother been out in the sun too long?*

"Miss Molly is going to need some new hair," Jackson told him as he whipped open the driver's-side door. "And Garrett is just the man to sew Miss Molly's new locks back onto her head. That would be *after* he stitches her head back fully onto her body."

For the first time since Autumn had rushed Blue off toward the house that morning, Tucker felt his heart lighten. Jackson's plan just might work. It had to. His little girl was counting on him to set things right.

An hour and a half later, all three Wade brothers were gathered around the examination table in Garrett's clinic, a small outbuilding that served as home base for his veterinary practice. Garrett, thank the good Lord, had been able to put Miss Molly back together again in an impressively neat and tidy manner. Most of the dirt had been scrubbed clean from her flimsy body and frilly dress. Her head had been firmly reattached. And while her neck was admittedly a little squattier as a result of the tussle she had been in with his horse, the slight imperfection was covered up by the brand-new much fuller head of hair their brother had so skillfully replaced.

"I can't believe I'm performing surgery on a doll,"

Garrett muttered with a shake of his head as he tied up the last stitch.

"Blue's doll," Jackson reminded him.

Tucker nodded.

His brother lifted his gaze to look at them. "You do realize that *she's* the only reason I'm doing this. Therefore, if word gets out and I start having little girls and their dolls lining up on my doorstep for repairs, the two of you are going to tend to them. Not me."

"Point made," Jackson said. "No one's going to find out about your baby doll doctoring skills from me. My lips are sealed."

"Same here." Tucker nodded in agreement.

"Good to know," Garrett said as he snipped off the piece of thread left dangling from the knot he'd just made. Then he took a step back to admire his handiwork. "There you go," he announced. "As good as new."

Tucker's throat clogged with emotion as he stood staring at the tiny rag doll. "Thank you," he muttered hoarsely. "Both of you." Things had seemed so hopeless when he'd finally gotten the doll back from Hoss. The frantic tug-of-war that had nearly separated Miss Molly's head from her body had left him fairly convinced that no amount of fervent prayer was going to be able to fix things. But his brothers hadn't given up hope and their faith had persevered.

"Well?" Garrett said.

Tucker looked up at his oldest brother.

"Are you just going to stand here admiring my handiwork, or are you going to take Miss Molly home where she belongs?"

He shifted uneasily. "We've still got work to do on the fence."

Jackson snorted. "A lot of help you'll be to us with your thoughts drawn back to those two pretty girls at the ranch."

"Jackson's right," Garrett told him, adding softly, "Go home."

Garrett cleaned up the snips of thread and strands of mop fibers from the examination table. "You need to be spending more time with Autumn, proving yourself worthy of her trust where her niece's happiness is concerned."

Tucker frowned. "Yeah, this morning was a good example of that. My horse ate her doll."

"Those things happen," his oldest brother replied. "I'm sure Autumn understands."

"What about Blue?" he demanded. "It might not be Autumn who throws up a roadblock when it comes to my getting custody of Blue. It might very well be my daughter. Especially after what happened this morning."

"She'll forget all about Hoss trying to eat Miss Molly after you return her baby doll to her," Jackson told him. "Besides, we're her family," he said as the three of them made their way out of the clinic. "Blue should be with us."

"Autumn is her family, too," Tucker reminded his brother with a sigh. "And Blue loves her aunt. How am I supposed to take my daughter away from the woman who helped raise her?"

Jackson pulled his car keys from his jeans pocket. "No way around it, Tucker. This is a rough situation. Someone's going to come out on the hurting end."

"That's what Autumn said," Tucker observed, his shoulders sagging under the weight of the situation.

"It's the truth," his brother continued. "But you're

Blue's father. You should've been the one helping to raise her all these years."

Garrett nodded in agreement as he walked them out to Jackson's truck. "Are you going to church Sunday?" Jackson asked.

"Can't say for sure," Tucker replied. "It depends on what Autumn and Blue are going to do. She didn't seem comfortable with it last week when I asked her and Blue to join me for Sunday services, which is why I went alone."

"Maybe now that they've been here for well over a week, Autumn will feel settled in enough to accept your invitation for her to join you for church."

"If they decline my offer to go to church this weekend, I'll probably stay home. I'd like to spend every moment I can with my daughter while she's here."

"It would be nice to have you all there."

He nodded. "I know, but I won't pressure Autumn into doing anything she's not completely comfortable with."

"You might find yourself rethinking that when the time comes for her to leave with your daughter," Jackson stated as he slid behind the steering wheel. "I suggest you take that gift you have with horses and use it to coax Autumn over to your way of thinking." That said, he closed the driver's-side door and started the truck.

Garrett accompanied his youngest brother the remainder of the way around to the passenger side. "Look, Tucker, I know this is a tough situation. Just know that whatever you need Jackson and I to do to help move matters along, all you have to do is ask."

Tucker opened the passenger door and then turned back to his brother. "I appreciate the support you and

Jackson have given me, despite my having disappointed the both of you by keeping my marriage to Summer from the family."

Garrett shrugged. "Can't change the past."

If only he could. "And I might take you up on your offer to help out. That is *if* I can convince Autumn to consent to spending some alone time with me after church on Sunday."

Garrett nodded. "Consider it done."

"Hopefully, it'll give her and me the time we need to iron some things out regarding custody of my daughter."

"There shouldn't even be any ironing required as far as I'm concerned," Jackson grumbled as he fastened his seat belt.

He glanced back over his shoulder at his brother. "I don't want this situation to become ugly. Autumn's got a lot to lose as well when all is said and done. So I'm hoping, with the good Lord's guidance, we'll be able to figure out a solution that works best for all involved in this tangle my wife created for us with her lies."

"Autumn should be thankful you're the kind of man you are," Jackson muttered. "Another man might not be so considerate of her feelings where Blue is concerned."

"She's not Summer," he said in Autumn's defense. "She's giving and selfless, and determined to do what's right when it comes to Blue. I won't hold her to blame for her sister's bad decisions."

"It's true. Autumn isn't Summer. You might want to keep that up front in your mind, little brother," Garrett warned with a studying glance.

"What exactly are you getting at?" Tucker asked as he hopped up into the truck.

"Autumn might not be Summer," his brother replied.

"But she is her identical twin. Don't let your heart confuse the two of them and risk losing what matters most when the time comes—Blue."

"Not a chance," Tucker replied, closing the door. His denial, however, didn't keep Autumn's sweet smile from drifting through his mind as they drove away.

"In here!" Autumn called out when she heard the front door open and close. She'd seen Tucker's truck coming up the drive from the living room window and had felt an unexpected stirring of excitement. It wasn't as if she'd been alone with nothing to do all day. She had been doing her best to keep Blue busy and her niece's thoughts away from the loss of her favorite doll. They'd watched a movie on Autumn's iPad, had colored for hours and were now entertaining Itty Bitty. So why then had she reacted to Tucker's coming home the way she had?

Before she could truly mull over that troubling thought, Tucker stepped into the room, his gaze searching until he found them seated on the floor in front of the fireplace where a flame burned low and warm. He immediately removed the cowboy hat from his head in a polite gesture, an action that came as no surprise at all to her. "Hello," she greeted with a tempered smile, not wanting him to know how ridiculously happy she was to see his grinning face.

"Daddy!" Blue exclaimed, jumping to her feet.

His daughter's warm welcome seemed to take Tucker off guard. Had he expected Blue to be upset with him for his horse's behavior that morning? Surely not. Hoss was a horse. He hadn't known better.

Tucker's gaze settled on the kitten purring loudly

in his daughter's arms. He blinked hard. And then he blinked again. "Is Bitty wearing a dress?"

His daughter offered up a toothy smile as she nodded her reply. "Isn't she pretty?"

"Uhm...yes, very pretty," he managed, his anxious gaze darting in Autumn's direction.

Autumn laughed softly. "Blue has decided to donate all of Miss Molly's dresses to Bitty after trying one on her for size and finding it a perfect fit."

"I see," he replied, his attention sliding back to the contented kitten. "Green seems to be her color." His gaze lifted once more to his daughter's face. "But I'm afraid Bitty might have to give one or two of her newly acquired dresses back to Miss Molly. We can't have your doll traipsing about the ranch in just one dress."

What did Tucker think he was doing? Autumn, who was no longer smiling, was tempted to lead him out into the hallway and ask him that very question. She had spent a good portion of that morning calming Blue down and helping her niece come to terms with the fact that her baby doll wasn't going to be riding back to Cheyenne with them when they left for home. And then Tucker comes home all smiles, acting as if nothing had ever happened. The fact that he had so quickly forgotten something that had been so emotionally devastating to his daughter was beyond disappointing.

"Tucker..." she began, trying to keep her voice unaffected by her irritation with his thoughtlessness. Only the remainder of her words caught in her throat as he reached into the hat that he had just removed and pulled out Blue's baby doll, which was, much to her shock, all in one piece!

"Miss Molly!" Blue cried out, immediately setting

the bedecked kitten down so she could go collect her precious doll.

Tucker handed the toy over to her, his grin widening as his daughter hugged it tight. "Miss Molly and I would've been home sooner, but we had a few fence posts that needed shoring up around the ranch first."

"She has white curls," Blue noted in confusion.

He exchanged a brief glance with Autumn before looking back down at his daughter. "She decided it was time for a change, so we got her hair done and came home to surprise you with it."

Blue lifted her gaze to his. "It's pretty. Can I get my hair done like hers?"

Tucker stammered, searching for a reply he clearly hadn't expected to give.

"Your hair is far too pretty to think about changing it," Autumn answered for him, feeling guilty for having immediately thought badly of him. It seemed there was a great deal of truth in the saying about old habits dying hard, her having spent the past several years thinking Tucker was the worst sort of man.

"Not to mention," Tucker joined in, "God chose that color especially for you so your hair can match your daddy's."

Blue's eyes narrowed as she studied Tucker's hair. "But you don't have any curls."

He ran a hand back through his thick, wavy hair. "If I let my hair grow out as long as yours is, you can bet there would be some curls."

She giggled at that. "Daddy, you can't have girl hair."

"A good thing," he told her. "It gets too hot when I'm out working the ranch to have anything but short hair under my cowboy hat."

"Will I have to wear a cowboy hat when I come to live here?"

"Only if you want to," he replied and then cast a worried glance in Autumn's direction.

She nodded, letting him know that it was okay. Blue had brought the subject up; Tucker hadn't. "You can worry about that later," Autumn told her.

"I have my uncles' hair, too," Blue said, shifting conversation gears once more.

"You do," Tucker said with a confirming nod. "We all get our hair color from your grandma Wade." Glancing past Blue, he nodded toward the assortment of coloring books lying open on the floor. "So what sort of mischief have you two girls been up to while I was away?"

"We were coloring with Bitty," Blue replied matter-of-factly.

Tucker's brow lifted, and Autumn had to suppress the urge to giggle at the bewildered expression on his face. "Your kitten can color?"

"Bitty can't hold a crayon," Autumn explained. "But she can help Blue pick out what color to use."

His gaze settled on the kitten that was playfully batting a lime-green crayon around on the floor in front of the fireplace where Autumn and Blue had been coloring. "She can, huh?"

Blue's head bobbed up and own. "I lay my crayons out on the floor and she sniffs the one I'm supposed to use next," she explained with adorable patience.

"Thus, the purple pumpkin in the princess's vegetable garden," Autumn said with a grin.

Tucker let out a husky chuckle, his own grin doing funny things to Autumn's heart. "I should have known

Itty Bitty was a very smart kitten when she chose my ranch house to be her new home."

"Box and all," Autumn agreed with a knowing grin.

"Do you wanna color with us?" Blue asked hopefully.

"It's been a while since I've colored," he admitted honestly. "Do you think Bitty might be willing to help me, too?" he asked as the dress-wearing kitten gave up its current source of entertainment to twine itself around Tucker's denim-clad leg.

"I'm thinking it might be time for Bitty to go outside for a spell," Autumn said. They had yet to pick up a litter box and she didn't want any accidents in the house. "I'll take her outside for a bit, but I'm quite sure Blue would be more than happy to help you pick colors."

"I could take her out," he offered, scooping the kitten up in his large sun-browned hand.

Autumn stepped over to ease Bitty from his gentle hold. Tucker deserved to spend some alone time with his little girl without her aunt continually hovering nearby. "I've got a few work calls I need to return," she told him. "That is, if you don't mind my leaving the two of you for a bit."

"Not at all," he said with a shake of his head. "Do what you need to do. Blue and I will make do until you can come back in and join us. Later, if you like, I could grill us up some burgers."

"With cheese?" Blue asked hopefully.

Autumn watched as that infamous Wade dimple cut into Tucker's tanned cheek with another one of his devastatingly handsome grins. "I think I can make that happen. Besides, what good is a burger without a big slab of cheese melted atop of it?"

He looked to the kitten in her arms. "Are you sure you don't want me to run her outside? It's a little chilly out."

"I'll throw on my jacket before I go out," she told him. "Besides, I think the two of you need a chance to spend some father-daughter bonding time together. But thank you for offering to include me in your coloring endeavors."

"I've told you before," he said, his green eyes locking with hers. "You're part of Blue's family. You're always going to be included in our lives."

She was beyond touched by his words, words she knew to be genuinely expressed. "Thank you for that, Tucker," she said softly. "It means a lot." She started for the door and then paused, glancing back over her shoulder at Tucker. "And burgers for dinner, ones oozing with cheese, sounds really good."

"You've got it," he said before turning away. She watched as he crossed the room to join Blue, who was already stretched out across the throw rug, surrounded by assorted coloring books and scattered crayons. Settling his large frame onto the floor across from his daughter, his back to Autumn, Tucker said, "All right, sweetheart, looks like it's just you and me."

"And Miss Molly," Autumn heard her niece say as she stepped from the room.

Looks like it's just you and me. Blue and her daddy. Just as Summer had wanted it to be. And judging by the effort Tucker was putting in to prove himself to be a good man and, more important, a good daddy, it seemed to be a part of the Lord's plan, as well.

Having enjoyed the cheeseburgers Tucker had promised to grill for them, he, Autumn and Blue had returned to the living room to spend a little quiet time before turning in for the night. His gaze drifted over to where Autumn sat in the matching rocker/recliner, flipping through the coloring book Blue had chosen for him to do his coloring in. She was smiling, looking completely relaxed. As if she belonged there, in his chair, his house, his life.

She's not Summer. Garrett had warned him to keep that first and foremost in his mind. And he had. At least, he thought he had. Why then did it feel so natural spending time with Autumn? Was it because she reminded him of his late wife? That same pretty, heart-shaped face. Same ice-blue eyes. Same slender build. But that was where the similarities ended. Summer had been harder around the edges. Autumn was softer, more open, more—

"Another trait my niece inherited from her father, I see," Autumn said with a smile, her head turning in his direction.

"Excuse me?"

She held up the open coloring book, pointing to a page where two little princesses were picking wildflowers in a field. "Blue's ability to stay within the line when coloring seems to have been inherited from her daddy's side, too. Just look at these cute little princesses you colored," she said, flashing him a playful grin.

"I had a good instructor." He glanced toward the sofa where Blue had fallen asleep shortly after they'd finished eating the cheeseburgers he'd grilled for them. His daughter looked so small as she lay curled up on her side beneath one of the blankets his mother had crocheted for him over the years. Her tiny mouth was lifted into a slight smile as she slept, as if dreaming of something that made her happy.

"I should probably put her to bed," Autumn said quietly. "But she looks so peaceful lying there."

"I was just thinking the same thing myself."

"I didn't have a chance to thank you earlier for saving Miss Molly."

He looked away, a frown tugging at his mouth. "Don't. It was my fault Miss Molly ended up being a chew toy for my horse. I should've known Hoss would be drawn to the doll."

"From experience?" she asked.

Tucker's head snapped back around. "What?"

"I'm not sure how you can take the blame for something you couldn't have known for certain would happen. That is, unless you make it a habit of carrying dolls out to the barn with you when you're seeing to your horses."

His smile eased its way back into place once more. "Can't say that I do."

"Then that settles it," she said. "You had no way of knowing Hoss has a thing for floppy old rag dolls."

"Well, I know now," he replied, keeping his voice low. "And you can rest assured that it'll never happen again."

"No doubt."

"You should have seen the tug-of-war Hoss and I had when I was trying to get Blue's doll back. He nearly tore poor Miss Molly's head off."

She glanced toward the doll, now all in one piece thanks to his brother's stitching skills, lying atop the blanket next to Blue. "She looks better than new." Glancing back at Tucker, she said, "Is there anything you can't do when you set your mind to it?"

He snorted. "A lot, I'm afraid. And I can't take credit

for the repairs that were done to Miss Molly. That honor would go to my brothers. Jackson came up with the idea to use a mop head to replace the doll's mangled hair. And Garrett did all the stitching."

"I'll be sure to thank them the next time I see them."

"You can thank them tomorrow," he told her. "That is, if you and Blue will consider joining us for church in the morning. We can swing by and grab lunch in town after Sunday service lets out."

She looked as if she were about to refuse his invitation.

"It would give you a chance to see a little bit of Bent Creek beyond the ranch," he added hopefully.

"You're forgetting that Blue and I made that emergency run into town to buy dinner the afternoon that I...um..."

"Burned the spaghetti?" he supplied with a grin.

She rolled her eyes, a faint blush filling her cheeks. "I'm never gonna live that down, am I?"

He chuckled softly. "Sooner or later, I suppose. Seriously, though, I'd like to show you around Bent Creek after church. Something beyond a quick trip to our local grocery store."

"I think that would be nice," she said and then sobered slightly. "I'm ashamed to admit that it's been far too long since I've attended church. Not since I was at Summer's memorial service."

Was her last memory of church too painful to bring herself to step into the Lord's house again? Or did she blame God for Summer's dying? Was that why she hadn't gone to church since her sister's passing? Whatever her reasons, Tucker didn't want to pressure her into anything she wasn't ready for. "If you'd rather not go, I understand."

"No," she said with a shake of her head, her gaze drifting over to her sleeping niece. "It's time. Not only for my sake, but for Blue's, as well."

He was glad to hear that. He wanted his daughter to be raised with the Lord being a very significant part of her life, just as He had been for Tucker and his brothers. "You'll have all of us there for support should you find yourself in need of it."

She gave an appreciative nod and then said with a halfhearted smile, "I can only pray that I will be strong enough not to need that support. Especially since I've already drenched one of your shirtfronts with my tears."

"Tears are a part of the healing process," he said softly. "And I have plenty of shirts to go around. You feel the urge, cry away." He didn't mean at that very moment, but it suddenly looked as if she were going to take him up on his offer.

"It's getting late," Autumn said, pushing out of the overstuffed recliner she'd been sitting in. "I should get Blue settled into bed if we're gonna make it to church in the morning."

Tucker stood, as well. "I need to go out and check on the horses before turning in for the night."

She started for the sofa, drawing his gaze to his sleepy little girl. "Here," he said, stepping up beside her. "Let me get her for you." He eased his hands under Blue's sleeping form, lifting her into his arms. Miss Molly tumbled from his daughter's limp hand.

"I've got her," Autumn said quietly as she bent to reach for the fallen doll baby.

They walked together until they reached the hallway, which was too narrow for them to walk comfortably side by side while Tucker was carrying Blue. He inclined his head with a smile. "After you."

Returning his smile, Autumn moved ahead of them. When she reached the guest room, she and Blue had been staying in, she opened the door and held it while Tucker carried his little girl inside. Then she hurried around him to draw the covers down.

Tucker lowered his daughter onto the mattress. Blue stirred, her eyes remaining closed as she murmured sleepily, "I love you, Daddy."

Tucker's heart slammed against his chest at those softly spoken words. Leaning in, he placed a tender kiss on his daughter's baby-soft cheek. "I love you, too, sweetheart." Then he straightened and turned to find Autumn watching him, moisture filling her eyes.

He felt like he needed to say something, but wasn't sure what that something should be. He settled for offering her a tender smile. "'Night, Autumn."

"'Night, Tucker," she said, looking as if she were about to say more. Instead, she turned away, fixing her watery gaze on Blue.

With one last glance at his daughter, Tucker strode from the room. But his little girl wasn't the only female filling his thoughts as he stepped out into the night to go check on his horses.

Chapter Seven

Sunday morning arrived, bringing with it a cloudless sky and the cheerful chirping of birds outside the bedroom window. The sound was soothing. Or had been before a loud rumbling along the drive outside put an end to the birds' sweet melodies.

Autumn stepped over to the bedroom window. Lifting the curtains aside, she watched as a large motor home bounced up and down and to and fro as it made its way up Tucker's somewhat uneven drive, leaving a trail of rising dust in its wake.

"Is it a train?" Blue asked from where she sat on the bed awaiting help with her tennis shoes.

"No, sweetie, it's not a train," she said as she stood peering outside.

"It sounds like one," her niece noted.

The oversize vehicle came to an abrupt stop in front of Tucker's house. "A train has to have tracks to travel on," Autumn explained somewhat distractedly, her gaze fixed on the goings-on outside. A man who looked to be in his mid- to late fifties leaped from the driver's side of the RV and raced around to open the passenger door, helping a slender auburn-haired woman down.

The woman, who looked to be slightly younger than the man assisting her, reached up to fuss with her short auburn curls as she looked anxiously toward the house. Then she slid her purse onto her arm, shoving the strap up over her shoulder, never missing a step as she hurried toward the house. The man kept pace beside her, looking every bit as anxious as she did.

He leaned in to say something to her and the woman nodded, slipping her arm through his as if for support.

Behind Autumn, Blue inquired with more persistence, "Was it thunder?"

She shook her head, her stomach twisting in a knot. Not thunder, but it could end up becoming an emotional thunderstorm. From the urgency in which the motor home had pulled in, and the anxious looks on the couples' faces, she had to assume Tucker had finally made that call to his parents.

No sooner had that thought crossed her mind than the barn door flew open and Tucker came striding out, his urgent, lengthy strides quickly eating up the distance between himself and his parents.

"No, sweetie," Autumn answered as she let the ruffled curtains fall back into place. Turning from the window, she crossed the room and hurried to buckle Blue's shiny black patent leather shoes. Thankfully, they were both dressed and ready for that morning's church service. It appeared her niece was about to make a very important first impression. "I believe we're about to have some very special company."

"Who is it?" Blue said, scooting off the foot of the bed where she'd been perched.

"I think I'll let your daddy introduce you." It was only right. With one last glance in the mirror to make certain she looked properly presentable to be meeting Tucker's parents, Autumn held out her hand to her niece. "Ready?"

Blue nodded. "Ready."

They made their way out of the guest room and down the hall just as the front door swung open and Tucker's momma stepped inside.

The older woman gasped. Her trembling hand flew to her mouth as she stood staring at her only grandchild, tears shimmering in her eyes.

Tucker's daddy stood a step behind her, his green eyes—eyes the same shade as Tucker's—widening and then welling up with unshed tears as he looked down upon his newfound granddaughter.

Tucker squeezed past their immobile forms and moved to stand beside Autumn and Blue. "Mom, Dad, I'd like you to meet your granddaughter, Blue Belle Wade." Then he knelt beside his daughter, saying in a voice filled with emotion, "Sweetheart, this is your grandma and grandpa Wade."

"The ones that have chickens?" Blue asked as she stood looking up at them.

Tucker chuckled, his gaze shifting to his parents. "We took a ride by your place to see your chickens."

"I got to put eggs in a basket," she told them excitedly and then held up a tiny hand with all five fingers extended. "Five of them. But one broke, so only four got to come home with us."

"She's precious," his momma sighed, clearly smitten already.

"And smart as a whip," his daddy boasted.

"She's a fast learner," Tucker agreed.

"She's got my smile," Mr. Wade added with a wide grin that displayed that infamous Wade dimple.

Tucker's momma moved to kneel in front of her granddaughter, tears in her eyes. "Hello, Blue."

"Why are you sad?" she asked worriedly as she looked up at her grandma.

"Oh, I'm not, honey," the older woman answered with a tender smile. "Not sad at all."

"But you're crying," Autumn's niece pointed out.

She laughed softly. "I suppose I am at that. But these are happy tears," she explained. "Very, very happy tears, because I finally get to meet my precious granddaughter. Do you think your grandma Wade might have a hug from you?"

Blue looked to Autumn.

"It's okay, sweetie," she told her niece with a reassuring smile. "Give your grandma a great big squeeze."

Tucker's momma held out her arms, and Blue stepped into them, wrapping her tiny arms around her grandma. More tears slid down the older woman's cheeks as the two embraced for the first time ever. "My sweet, sweet baby," she said.

"But I'm not a baby," Blue said somewhat defensively.

Tucker's momma loosened her hold and leaned back to look at Blue. "Of course, you're not. You're a big girl. One I am so very happy to finally have a chance to meet. You look so pretty all dressed up in your Sunday best."

"Thank you," Blue said almost shyly.

"If you have a spare hug to give," Tucker's daddy said, kneeling next to his wife and Blue, "your grandpa wouldn't mind having one, too."

This time Blue didn't look to Autumn. Instead, she re-leased her hold on Tucker's momma to hug her grandpa."

When the embrace ended, Tucker's daddy stood, help-ing his wife to her feet. Then he cleared his throat and looked away.

"Dad?" Tucker said worriedly. "Everything okay?"

"Never been better. Just got a speck of something in my eye," he muttered as he swiped a hand over the tear-dampened lashes Autumn had glimpsed before the man had turned away.

Autumn felt her own tears building as she looked on. The older couple's joy was palpable. There was no denying their welcoming acceptance of Blue as their grandchild, despite the lengthy delay in their finding out about her. Precious years Summer had taken away from them they could never get back. Autumn had to wonder if they would harbor resentment toward her for the actions her sister had taken since Summer was no longer able to be held accountable for what she'd done.

"Mom, Dad," Tucker said, drawing everyone's atten-tion as he motioned toward Autumn, "I'd like for you to meet Blue's aunt. Miss Myers is Summer's twin sister."

Was, Autumn thought sadly, but now wasn't the time or place to point that out. She greeted his parents with a warm smile. "It's a pleasure to finally meet you, Mr. and Mrs. Wade."

"Emma, please," his momma insisted. Then she cast a chastising glance her son's direction, muttering, "And *finally* is right. You've known about my grandbaby for twelve days and last night was the first time you saw fit to call us?"

"Now, honey," his daddy said soothingly, not that Tucker's momma sounded angry with her son as much as hurt. "Tucker explained his reasons for not calling us right away. Our son's heart was in the right place, even if we would have preferred to hear about our granddaughter the second her existence was made known to him." He turned to Autumn, and then, taking a step forward, surprised her completely by giving her a big, warm, welcoming bear hug. "God bless you, Miss Myers," he said, his voice choked with emotion.

As soon as he released her, Emma Wade gathered Autumn into what could only be described as a motherly hug, not that she'd ever been on the receiving end of one of those from her own mother. "Our family will forever be grateful to you for what you've done for our son. For all of us," she said, looking to Blue.

She hadn't done anything yet, Autumn wanted to tell them. No decision had been made with regard to Blue. She'd brought her niece there because it was the right thing to do. Not only to follow through with Summer's last request, but because Blue deserved to know that part of her family. But she wasn't anywhere near mentally prepared to turn her niece over to someone else's care.

"Do you have any kitties?" Blue asked, looking up at her grandparents.

Tucker's momma released Autumn and smiled adoringly down at her granddaughter. "Lots of them as a matter of fact. They like to stay near the barn, chasing field mice."

"Where the horses are?" her niece asked uneasily.

Tucker's parents exchanged glances at Blue's wide-eyed response to her grandma's reply.

"Blue's a little wary of horses," he explained as gently as he could, seeing as how a full explanation wasn't possible with Blue standing right there.

"Do your kitties have a house like the chickens get to sleep in?" her niece went on, thankfully far too distracted by thoughts of kittens to let memories of her momma's accident invade the special moment.

Emma Wade's smile widened. "I suppose they do, if you count the barn. That's where they spend most of their time."

"Do you make cookies?"

"I have three boys," his momma answered. "Making cookies comes with being their mother."

Blue's face lit up. "What kind of cookies?"

"All kinds," her niece's newly discovered grandmother answered. "Chocolate chip, iced sugar cookies, kiss cookies and oatmeal raisin to name a few. Do you like cookies?"

Autumn watched her niece's head bob up and down quite enthusiastically. "I like peanut butter cookies," she told her grandma.

"Then we'll just have to see about making you some."

"Maybe you can help Grandma Wade make a batch after we get home from church," Blue's grandpa suggested and then looked to Autumn. "That is, if it's okay with your aunt."

"You're going to church?" Tucker said in surprise.

His momma looked his way. "When have you known your father and I not to attend Sunday services? We would've gone to one we found in Jackson, but after your call last night all we could think about was getting home to see our grandbaby. We packed up our campsite last evening and started for home before daybreak this morning." Her attention shifted back to Blue and her expression softened even more. "I have every intention of sitting in church today with my family and thanking the good Lord for blessing us with this beautiful little girl. Even if my clothes do look a little travel weary, I'm sure the good Lord will forgive me."

"If we don't get a move on, there won't be any forgiveness needed," Tucker's daddy said with a grin.

Tucker nodded, his gaze shifting to Autumn. His expression grew serious. "You and Blue ready?"

She wasn't certain whether he was referring to their being ready for that morning's church services or for the addition of more family to Blue's life, but she knew there was no turning back either way. If Blue were to end up living in Bent Creek, she wanted to get to know the people her niece would be surrounded by, the church she would build her faith in, the town she would become a part of. That didn't make any of this any easier. Each step toward a new life for Blue made Autumn feel the impending loss of her own happiness even greater. *Dear Lord, continue to give me the strength to do the right thing.*

With a slow nod, she said, "I'll just go grab our coats." Then Autumn set off back down the hall to the guest room she'd been sharing with Blue, thankful for a few moments alone to collect her emotions and prepare for the changes that were yet to come in her and Blue's lives.

Tucker watched as his parents whisked Blue away from the restaurant they had gone to eat lunch at after church, the three of them piling into his parents' RV to go back to their house and help her grandma bake cookies. His brothers were already on their way there and would, no doubt, hang around until the baking was done. They never missed out on a freshly made batch of his mother's cookies.

Beside him, Autumn stood watching as well, almost longingly as she tucked her coat tighter about herself.

"We could go with them," he suggested, not wanting her to feel ill at ease by Blue's going off without her. "I know it's gotten colder." A front had moved in while they were attending services, causing the temperatures to drop. Billowy gray clouds filled the afternoon sky, effectively blocking the sun's warming rays.

"I don't mind a little cold," she said, turning to face him.

"If you're sure."

"I'm sure," she said with another glance in the direction Blue had gone with his parents.

"Maybe about braving the weather," he said, "but I'm not so certain you're comfortable with your decision to allow Blue to go home with my family."

She looked up at him, managing a smile. "I wouldn't have agreed if I was at all uncomfortable. It's just hard seeing my niece ride away without me, but Blue needs to spend some time with her grandparents and her uncles without my intrusion. Besides, I'm looking forward to seeing more of Bent Creek with you. Thank you again for offering to give me a tour."

"First of all," he said, "you are *not* an intrusion. And secondly, I should be thanking you, not the other way around. Or, at the very least, apologizing."

Confusion filled those thickly-lashed silver-blue eyes of hers. "Apologizing for what?"

His mind went blank as he took in her pretty upturned face. The sunlight made the blue of her eyes look more like liquid crystals, while the brisk fall air added a touch of color to her cheeks.

"Tucker?"

Her sweet voice had him shaking off the unexpected reverie and focusing on what she'd asked him. "I'm sorry about my parents' surprise visit this morning," he answered. "If I had known they were coming, I would have given you a heads-up to prepare for…well, their excitement."

"They were that," she said, laughing softly.

"No kidding," he added, his own laughter joining hers. "I thought a herd of elephants was stampeding their way up the drive when I was in the barn this morning."

"Your daughter thought it was a train," she said. "I don't think I've ever seen a motorhome move at that rate of speed before. At least, not down a dirt-and-gravel road." Her smile changed suddenly, giving way to a fretful frown.

"Autumn?"

She looked up with a worried expression. "Tucker, please tell me your daddy doesn't normally drive as fast as he did this morning."

"He wasn't going as fast as you might have thought he was," he told her, wanting to set her mind at ease. "Even a slight increase in speed in an RV as it's traveling over an uneven road like the one coming up to the house is bound to make the vehicle's approach appear more reckless than it actually is. I promise you, Blue is in good hands with my family."

Her pretty features eased with his reassurance.

"Truth is, my parents thought they might never have grandchildren."

"They have three sons," she said. "Why would they think that?"

"Because I had no inclination to marry, for reasons they didn't know at the time. Garrett was head over heels for a girl he dated all through high school, but she got sick their junior year and ended up dying the following year of leukemia. He's never dated anyone seriously since then."

"That's so heartbreaking."

He nodded. "I don't think Garrett ever really got over losing her."

"And Jackson?"

"He was a real ladies' man until several years ago when the nearly two-thousand-pound bull he was riding threw him to the ground and then trampled him, crushing his hip and his leg in the process," he said with a frown. "He hasn't dated since."

"That's why he limps," she said in understanding.

"Yes. There was a time the doctors didn't know if he would ever be able to walk on that leg again."

"Your poor brothers."

"Enough about my brothers," he said. "Let's get on with that walk I promised you."

They started down the sidewalk, Autumn's curious gaze taking in the town around her as they went. She noted that, like the town she had grown up in, all but a few of the storefronts were occupied. A sign that Bent Creek was thriving economically.

In the center of town, a monument surrounded by neatly trimmed shrubs stretched up toward the sky. "Eighteen twenty-eight," Autumn said, reading the raised date that ran down the stone pillar.

"The year Bent Creek was first founded," Tucker explained. "The town is small with our population here being just under five thousand, but we've got a lot of the modern conveniences you'd find in a bigger town. A feed store, a leather and boot store, a full-service auto parts store, a local rodeo, not to mention the best fishing around."

Humor lit her eyes. "I see. All the things a nearly five-year-old girl would wanna have in her life."

His smile sagged. How had he not given more thought to what he was saying when trying to sell Autumn on all the positive things his town offered? Of course, a young girl didn't care about a boot store or how reasonably priced an oil change was.

Autumn reached out, placing a gentle hand on his arm. "Tucker, I'm only teasing. Looking around, I can see Bent Creek has a lot to offer Blue. A library, a local art gallery and even a YMCA. Do they have a pool?"

He nodded. "They do."

"That's good to know. Blue loves to swim."

Tucker made a quick mental note of that. "Does she like donuts?"

"She does. All things sweet, in fact," she said and then added reflectively, "Just like her momma used to."

He remembered that about his wife and wondered if having a sweet tooth could be genetic. "Well, we've got a donut shop at the far end of town that serves up some of the best coffee in the county." He paused and then muttered with a knowing frown, "Not that Blue would care one iota about the quality of their coffee." Was he ever going to get this parenting thing right?

"Probably not," Autumn agreed with an empathetic smile, making him wonder if he'd spoken that last thought aloud. "But I'll bet they serve hot chocolate there, as well," she continued, confirming that his fear of failure as a parent wasn't what she'd been referring to.

He nodded. "They do."

"Good hot chocolate?" she asked almost longingly,

making Tucker wonder if Autumn Myers had a sweet tooth herself.

Truth was Tucker found himself wondering a lot of things about his daughter's aunt. Like her favorite color, where she'd liked to travel to if given the chance and if she missed living in Texas. He already knew she was loving and giving, and possessed a strength of character that ran deeper than most. She had overcome an emotionally painful upbringing, yet still strove hard to focus on the positive things in her life. He couldn't help but admire Autumn for that. It was something he wished he were better at doing.

Tucker smiled, feeling more at ease with Autumn than he had with any woman since he'd left Cheyenne. "Why don't we get a couple of cups of it to go before we head back to the ranch for your tour there and you can judge for yourself?"

"I would love to get some hot chocolate," she said with a sigh. "It's always been a weakness of mine. Just ask my best friend, Hope. We used to drink it at every sleepover we had. With mini marshmallows if some were available."

More bits and pieces of her life Autumn was choosing to share with him. Her willingness to open up to him in that way meant a lot to Tucker. "Then we definitely need to get you some."

They worked their way along the sidewalk lining one side of town while Tucker told her a little bit more about Bent Creek's history.

"You know so much about this place."

"I should," he told her. "I grew up here."

"No," she said. "It's more than that. It's clear just listening to you talk that you have a deep-rooted love of this tiny town."

He nodded. "I suppose I do. But I have to admit it took my going away, riding the circuit and living elsewhere to make me realize what I had left behind."

"They do say that home is where the heart is," she said, looking away.

"I take it yours is still back in Texas."

She shrugged. "At one time. But then I discovered that my heart is wherever my niece is. So it appears that old saying might not always ring true, because my home might not be where my *heart* is one day soon."

His heart went out to her, but they both knew the outcome of their situation was going to leave someone hurting. And it seemed it would be her. Apparently, he was succeeding in winning her over, which was what he'd set out to do. So why then did it feel as if he were losing at that same time? "When Blue comes to live here—"

"If," she corrected, shoring up her shoulders.

So, she wasn't completely sold yet. He could accept that. Yet, the possibility of Autumn deciding Blue was not better off in his care, forcing him to seek legal means to gain custody of his daughter, had Tucker frowning. The last thing he wanted to do was go to battle against Autumn over his daughter, but he would if it came down to a choice between a life with or without her in it.

Autumn sighed. "I suppose while I'm putting myself out there, I might as well admit that you're doing a surprisingly good job of convincing me that Blue might just be better off here with her daddy and his large, loving family. Might," she reiterated.

Her words lifted a huge weight from his shoulders. "I wouldn't expect you to make your decision just yet. Not until you've had a chance to see more of who I am and what I do. Today—" he glanced up at the ever-darkening sky "—if the weather holds, you'll get to see more of the ranch, including the broncs and their weanlings."

"Weanlings?"

He looked back at her with a smile. "Little ones. They'll be out stretching their legs. We'll just have to find them. And if you have any questions about what I do, feel free to ask as we go."

"You can count on it," she said. "Because that all comes into play as well in my decision. I intend to take everything I've seen and learned while staying here into consideration. I just hope…" Her words trailed off.

"What do you hope?" he asked.

"That you're truly in this for the long haul," she told him. "Because raising a child is a lifetime commitment."

"I have every intention of loving and cherishing, and seeing to the raising of my daughter until my last breath," he told her, meaning it with all his heart. "How could I consider doing anything less? Blue is a blessing from God. One whose very existence in this world has made me what I never even knew I longed to be until she came into my life—a father."

"You'd be surprised how many men there are who don't share your sentiments," she said, her words catching slightly.

Regret filled him. How could he have been so insensitive in his choice of words? Not when she'd told him about her own father's abandonment after learning about the double blessing God had bestowed upon him. "Autumn…"

She held up a hand to cut off his apology. "Please don't. You and I know there's no changing the past, as much as we'd long to be able to. But we can make certain Blue never feels like she was set aside by either of us, no matter what the outcome may be."

"Agreed," he said with a determined nod.

They walked in silence for several long moments before Autumn said, "I enjoyed the Sunday service today."

"I'm glad. It was nice having you and Blue accompany me," Tucker replied, grateful that Autumn had redirected their conversation. Her past made him angry on her behalf, made his heart hurt for her, made him wish there were something he could do to right the wrongs done to her in her life. But she was correct. There was no changing the past. Not for any of them.

"It was nice being there," she admitted with a soft smile. "And Reverend Walker's sermon was really uplifting. I can see why the place was so packed."

The church had been filled to capacity that morning, but that was pretty much the norm. "Being introduced to so many people had to be a little overwhelming for you. Maybe even awkward," he added, "considering the curious glances that kept coming our way."

"I didn't mind," she said, setting his mind at ease. "Not really. I wanna know the people my niece might be surrounded by if she were to come live here with you. Their curiosity is completely understandable, seeing as how you introduced Blue to them as your daughter with no time to really explain how that came about."

"I suppose I should prepare myself for the whole truth to come out," he said with a sigh.

"Tucker, it's not your fault the marriage failed," she said, surprising him with her words of support.

"Sometimes I wonder," he said solemnly.

"I know my sister…knew," she corrected sadly, "and

aside from the fact that she had a tendency to be impulsive with some very important decisions in her life, I think fear drove her away from you."

"Fear?" he repeated. "You think Summer was afraid of me?"

"Not at all," she didn't hesitate to respond. "I think she was afraid the past would repeat itself, and, like our folks had done, you would abandon her just like our daddy did our momma once you'd learned about the baby."

"I never gave Summer any reason to believe—"

"You didn't have to," she told him. "It was already rooted deep inside of her. Our daddy wanted nothing to do with our momma once he'd learned she was carrying his child...children, actually. Maybe the thought of having two babies at once, when he wasn't prepared for even one, was enough to send him running. Then Momma did pretty much the same thing. Maybe she was overwhelmed. Maybe she resented us for our daddy's leaving. Whatever the case, I think Summer pulled away from you before she could be the one left hurting again."

He hadn't considered that, but then it was hard to get past the bitterness he'd felt toward Summer for so long. Autumn had a way of putting things into perspective when it came to her life. To Summer's life. "How is it you are so different from your sister? And I don't mean that in a bad way. Just honest."

"The Lord gives us the choice to either focus on the bad in our lives, or on the blessings we've been given," she explained. "I try to focus on the good, no matter how bad things get. Even if it's not always possible to do so. But Summer was never able to push away the bad."

He glanced her way. "You're a very special woman, Autumn Myers. I hope you know that."

She glanced away, as if she'd been made uncomfortable by his compliment. But he didn't regret giving it. She was special. However, he decided to direct their conversation to something far less personal.

They crossed a side street to the corner Abby's Donuts sat on. Tucker's gaze was drawn to the donut shop's large storefront windows that lined that side of the building. "The good news about coming here after church," he said, "is that it's nowhere near as busy as it is before church when people are stopping in to get their morning coffee and a quick bite to eat." He reached for the door, but it opened before his hand could come to rest on the handle, forcing him to take a step back.

Justin Dawson, Bent Creek's sheriff and his brother Jackson's best friend, offered a nod of greeting. "Tucker." Then he stopped dead in his tracks as his gaze landed on Autumn, who stood next to Tucker on the sidewalk.

"Justin," Tucker said, returning the nod. "Missed you at church this morning."

"I'm on duty," he replied distractedly. "Just stopped in for a quick cup of coffee." Curiosity lit his eyes as he tipped his hat to Autumn. "Ma'am."

Realizing he'd neglected to make introductions, Tucker said, "Autumn Myers, this is Sheriff Dawson."

"Justin," he countered as he extended a hand in greeting. "An old family friend of the Wades."

She accepted the offered hand with a warm smile. "It's a pleasure to meet you, Justin."

Tucker gritted his teeth, suddenly feeling the need to list all the reasons why it shouldn't be a pleasure for her to meet Justin. But the man really had no faults big enough to lay out there that would make a difference. And why did it matter? Autumn was free to smile at any man she pleased. Even if it suddenly didn't please Tucker.

"Pardon my surprise," Justin said as he released her hand, "but I can't say that I've ever seen Tucker parading a female around town, let alone one as pretty as you."

She blushed at the compliment. Then again, the color in her cheeks might have been from the damp chill filling the air. Tucker decided to go with the latter. Autumn was, as she put it herself, a reasonable woman. One who clearly knew not to be drawn in by his friend's flirtatious words. At least, he hoped that were the case.

"You haven't seen me 'parading' anyone around, because I believe in holding to the vows I made when I got married," Tucker countered with a frown.

Justin's head snapped around so fast it was a wonder he didn't suffer whiplash. "Excuse me?"

Tucker sighed. This wasn't how he'd planned on letting the truth out to close friends, but there it was. "The reason you haven't seen me with another female is because I got married when I was riding the rodeo circuit several years back."

"You're married?"

"Not any longer," he replied.

"Why don't I go on in and get the hot chocolate?" Autumn suggested, clearly uncomfortable by the turn their conversation had taken. "Give you two a chance to speak in private."

"You sure?" Tucker asked worriedly, searching her gaze.

"I think I can manage to pick a few donuts out all by myself," she told him with a reassuring smile.

"This talk can wait until a better time," Justin insisted. "You two go ahead and enjoy your afternoon."

"You've already said you're a close friend of the family," Autumn told him. "I don't mind Tucker taking a moment to explain to you what's going on in his life." She turned back to Tucker. "What kind of donut would you like?"

He pulled his wallet from the back pocket of his jeans and withdrew a twenty-dollar bill, holding it out to her. "I don't have a preference. Just grab me whatever catches your fancy. I won't be long."

She nodded, her attention shifting back to Justin. "If you'll excuse me."

He gave a polite nod, not that Autumn would have seen it. She had already turned away, disappearing into the donut shop, the door drifting shut behind her.

Tucker watched her go, knowing that he could have handled things better when it came to telling Justin he was, or at least had been, married. But seeing his friend smiling at Autumn the way he had been, well, it mattered. Even when it shouldn't.

"I'm sorry if I stepped into something I shouldn't have," his friend said. "Jackson never made mention of your being married. Neither did Garrett for that matter."

He turned to look at his friend. "It's not your fault. No one knew. Not even my family."

"You eloped?"

"We did," he confirmed. "But things didn't work out the way my wife hoped they would and she chose to walk away. Only she failed to tell me that she was carrying my child at the time."

Justin's jaw dropped. "*You* have a child?"

Tucker nodded. "A daughter. One I only just found out about. Blue's four, almost five."

"Close to Lucas's age," he noted, referring to his nephew. "He'll be seven in December. So how did you find out about…Blue, wasn't it?"

"Blue Belle Wade," he acknowledged with a father's deep-felt pride. "Autumn brought her here to meet me after my wife, her sister, confessed what she had done, something she only did to set things right with the Lord before dying."

"Your wife died?"

"Six months ago." He went on to explain the events that had transpired and how he was doing everything he could to prove to Autumn that his daughter belonged with him.

"You're a good man, Tucker," his friend said. "Everyone in Bent Creek knows that. And if it comes down to a court battle I'm willing to testify on your behalf. Just say the word."

"I appreciate that, Justin. However, I'm hoping Autumn and I can work things out without having to go the route of a messy court battle."

"I hope she feels the same way," he said, taking a drink of coffee from the cup he'd carried out with him.

"I know she doesn't want to put Blue through any more undue stress. She loves my daughter like she was her own," he told Justin. "Not surprising since Autumn helped to raise Blue. I believe in my heart she'll do what's best for her, whatever that may end up being."

"I can understand her not wanting to put your daughter under any more stress," his friend said with a heavy sigh. "Lainie and her son are still struggling to come to terms with Will's death and it's been nearly eight months."

Lainie was Justin's little sister. A widow at the ripe young age of twenty-eight. Her husband, Will, had died after their car was struck by a drunk driver. "I take it you still haven't been able to convince her to move back to Bent Creek yet?"

He shook his head. "Mom and Dad and I have all tried. Lainie's determined to stay in Sacramento, wanting to keep Lucas's life as close to normal as possible given the circumstances." He met Tucker's gaze. "But I'm still worried about her."

"Understandable. But your sister's a grown woman. All you can do right now is continue to let her know there's a place for them back here if she decides Sacramento isn't where they need to be."

"I intend to," he said with a troubled frown. "I just wish my sister was here where I could lend her a hand, even offer her a shoulder to cry on if she needs it."

Tucker glanced toward the front window where inside he could see Abby, the owner of Abby's Donuts, filling a pastry box with Autumn's selections. "I'm sure Lainie knows her family is only a phone call away."

"I suppose so," he said. "Speaking of family, is yours planning on attending this year's fall barbecue?"

"They never miss it." The town's annual barbecue was a big event. Most of Bent Creek attended the festivities. Grills were set up just outside the enclosed pavilion at the town's park and ribs were brought in, along with Abe Johnson's specialty barbecue sauce. Everyone brought covered dishes and their own tableware. And there was always some sort of musical entertainment planned for that afternoon's events.

"What about you? Will you be there?"

Tucker shrugged. "I'm not sure what my plans are yet. It all depends on how long Autumn and Blue will be staying here."

"If they're still here, then bring them along," Justin suggested. "Kids love picnics. Even if they're inside. Especially when there's a table set up specifically for desserts."

"I'll be sure to use that as my selling point," he said with a chuckle.

"Seriously though," the sheriff said, "I hope to have a chance to meet this little girl of yours before she goes back to Cheyenne."

"I'd like that, too," Tucker had no sooner said when the skies above let loose a mixture of both rain and snow. He reached for the door. "And, Justin…"

"Yes?"

"If you don't mind, could you keep Blue and I in your prayers?"

"You don't even have to ask," his friend said with a farewell nod before striding away.

Tucker stepped into the donut shop and removed his cowboy hat, shaking off the slushy drops that had accumulated atop it before moving farther inside. Hat in hand, he made his way up to the counter where Autumn was paying for the donuts and hot chocolate she had purchased.

"There's one of my favorite customers," Abby said with her usual playful greeting.

Autumn glanced back over her shoulder, her gaze coming to rest on Tucker. A slender brow lifted. "Favorite, huh?"

He chuckled as he moved to stand beside her. "Okay, so I confess. I might have a bit of a sweet tooth myself."

"And here I was thinking you came by so often just to see me," Abby said, feigning disappointment as she handed Tucker the box of donuts Autumn had selected.

Abby was at least ten years older than his mother, so Tucker knew she was only teasing him. That and the fact that she was already happily married to her husband of forty-plus years. A part of him wished he had managed to find the kind of long-lasting love Abby and his own parents had. The other part of him, the part in charge of sound reasoning, said a forever-kind-of-love hadn't been part of God's plan for him.

Autumn's gaze moved past him to the window. "Oh, no," she gasped. "It's raining."

"Sleeting, actually," he told her as he tucked the box under the crook of his arm. "Looks like our tour of the ranch will have to wait until tomorrow."

He'd be lying to himself if he didn't admit that it pleased him to see the disappointment that registered on her face with his announcement. It meant that Autumn had been looking forward to their outing and learning more about the business he and his brothers ran.

She glanced once more toward the sleet-splattered windowpanes and then turned back to him, a sweet smile moving across her pretty face. "Until tomorrow, then."

Tucker found himself wishing their tour didn't have to wait. Surprisingly, he was eager to share that part of his life with Autumn. For Blue's sake, of course. At least, that was what he was trying very hard to convince himself of.

Chapter Eight

Tucker pulled up to his house, his mouth caught up in a wide grin. The cold front from the day before had long since passed. The afternoon sun shone brightly in the cloudless sky above. Even the temperature had risen, making it feel more like a September afternoon than a mid-October one. He couldn't have asked for a more perfect day to tour his and his family's ranches.

He was about to go fetch Autumn and Blue when they stepped out onto the porch, offering waves of greeting. His daughter was dressed in blue jeans and her fall coat. She was wearing the pale pink cowgirl boots Tucker had bought for her. The ones with the tiny silver, glittery stars on the outer sides of the boots' shafts. Autumn was in jeans as well, but instead of cowgirl boots she wore hikers that were both stylish and low-heeled enough to be practical for the outing they had planned. Not that his daughter's aunt wasn't quite skilled when it came to moving about in heels of any height.

It took a moment for it to dawn on him that Autumn was lugging Blue's car seat with her. He mentally kicked himself for being so distracted by Autumn's choice of footwear that he hadn't even thought to jump out and retrieve it from her. He was out of the truck and moving toward her in long, hurried strides.

Blue skipped ahead of her aunt. "Hi, Daddy!"

"Hi, sweetheart," he replied, his heart swelling as it did every time his daughter called him Daddy. His gaze lifted to Autumn's pretty face and he gave a slight nod. "Afternoon. Here," he said, reaching for the seat, "let me get that for you."

"Thank you," she said, relinquishing her hold on it.

They walked to his vehicle where Tucker placed the seat inside the back of the roomy cab and then attempted to secure it properly. Only he couldn't figure out exactly how to do so. If only he had paid more attention when Autumn had done this before.

For a moment, Tucker considered winging it and then decided it was better to admit his inability to perform the task at hand than to take even the slightest risk with his daughter's safety. Glancing back at Autumn with a frustrated frown, he said, "I can saddle a horse, but I can't figure out how to buckle in a car seat."

She smiled in response as she stepped up beside him to demonstrate. "I was the same way at first. You'll learn."

He would learn. Her words gave him more hope that his daughter would soon be living with him. Bending, he scooped Blue up and placed her into the car seat Autumn had managed to secure.

"Do you need help?" Autumn asked from behind him.

"Thanks, but I can at least handle this part." He gave the shoulder harness belt a tug to make certain it was firmly latched in. "Are you ready to go see Daddy's other horses?" he asked Blue, unable to deny his own excitement. He'd been wanting to do this for a while, but had waited until he felt Blue was ready. Her growing interest in Hoss and Little Joe and her willingness to be near them convinced him it was time to see how she did around the rest of the horses.

His daughter's head gave a slow bob up and down. "Can we go see the butterflies, too?"

"We'll have to do that another day when you're both wearing your tennis shoes. We wouldn't want those pesky little stones scratching up your and your aunt Autumn's pretty shoes."

"Then can we go to my grandma and grandpa's after we see the horses?"

Tucker's smile softened even more. Blue had taken to her grandparents like a honeybee to a brightly blooming flower. "I think we can make that happen if it's all right with your aunt."

Blue tipped forward to see past his large frame. "Can we, Aunt Autumn?"

"If time allows. We wouldn't wanna interrupt their dinner."

"Okay," his daughter said, settling back against her car seat, seemingly satisfied by her aunt's response.

Tucker stepped back and closed the passenger door. Then he looked to Autumn. "I think we're ready." Reaching past her, he opened her door and then helped her up into the truck's cab before making his way around to the driver's side.

"Don't forget what I said about asking questions if there's something you'd like to know," Tucker said as he settled behind the steering wheel. Putting the truck in gear, he pulled away from the house.

A short distance down the road that ran past all of

his family's ranches, Blue exclaimed, "Look at all the big brown chickens!"

Tucker glanced out Autumn's window, chuckling as he spied the flock of wild turkeys his daughter had caught sight of. "Those are turkeys. They run wild in these parts."

"Do they lay brown eggs?"

"More of a beige," he answered. "They're bigger than the eggs a chicken lays, and are usually speckled."

They came over a rise, and Blue's attention shifted elsewhere. "Tiny horses!"

Autumn gasped as she watched the young horses race across the range. "They're adorable." She looked to Tucker. "I take it those are the weanlings."

He nodded.

"That's the main barn up ahead," he said, indicating the large building that sat off to one side in the distance.

"I remember seeing it when we stopped by your momma and daddy's to collect eggs that day."

"It's the largest of all our barns and was already set up with fencing to hold a lot more horses. We use it to store grain, equipment for training green horses, rodeo equipment, those kinds of things. The horses themselves are free range."

"Meaning?" Autumn asked.

"Meaning they spend their days and nights out on the range."

"Don't they get cold?" Blue asked.

Tucker met his daughter's questioning gaze in the rearview mirror. "No, sweetheart, they don't. Broncs are strong and adaptable, and made to survive in this kind of country whatever the weather."

"It's back," Blue said.

"What's back?" Autumn asked.

"The bee," his daughter replied. "I hear it buzzing again."

Again? It was too cold for bees. How could… Tucker suddenly recalled having left his cell phone in the pocket of the coat he'd been wearing when he went out to work that morning. As the day had warmed up, he'd switched to a lightweight jacket he kept in the back seat of his truck.

"That would be my phone." He pulled over, placing the truck in Park. Then he jumped out and opened the passenger door. Reaching into the coat's pocket, he pulled out his cell phone which, at this point, had stopped ringing.

Tucker pulled up the missed call list to find that he hadn't answered several calls from the nursing home. Concern filled him. "Excuse me a moment," he said apologetically to Autumn and his daughter. "I need to make a call."

Closing the truck's door, he returned the call.

"Sunny Days Nursing Home," a woman answered. "Susan speaking. How may I help you?"

"Susan," he said, "Tucker Wade calling. Someone there has been trying to reach me."

"That was me," she said, sounding relieved.

"Is it Wylie?" he asked worriedly, praying complications from his recent surgery hadn't set in.

"I'm afraid so," she replied. "He woke up from a nap disoriented and has been out of sorts ever since. We were wondering if you might be available to come by and see if you can settle him down before we have to call the doctor in."

He glanced toward the truck where Autumn and Blue

waited for him. Once again, their tour was going to have to wait. Maybe the good Lord was trying to tell him something. Like giving Autumn a glimpse of who he was might not be in his best interest. But he couldn't figure out why that would be. "I'll be there in about twenty minutes." As soon as he swung by and dropped Autumn and Blue off at the house.

Guilt stabbed at Tucker as he settled in behind the truck's wheel and started the engine.

"Tucker," Autumn said worriedly. "Is everything okay?"

"A friend needs me. It's nothing to worry yourself over," he said as he turned the truck around. Glancing her way, he added with a sigh, "But I'm afraid we're going to have to put off our tour until I get back."

"You're leaving?"

"There's something I need to see to that can't wait. I'll drop you and Blue off at the ranch on my way. I'm not sure how long I'll be gone, but I'm hoping it won't be too long." He didn't see any need to get into the details. Telling Autumn about Old Wylie would only bring back sad memories of her own grandma's failing health before she'd passed.

"No grandma's?" Blue said with a pout.

He hated disappointing his daughter, but this couldn't be helped. "We'll head back out when I get home and finish our tour. Afterward we'll stop by and visit with Grandma and Grandpa Wade."

Autumn tried not to show her displeasure with Tucker's abrupt change of their plans. One he didn't care to offer an explanation for, other than a friend needed him. Well, his daughter needed him, too. Blue had been so excited to go on a tour of her daddy's ranch and see the weanlings. It was still hard to believe how much she had overcome since arriving there, most notably her intense fear of horses. Not that her niece's uneasiness when it came to the four-legged, doll-swiping creatures was completely diminished. But with Tucker's help, Blue had made great strides in reconnecting with her love of horses again.

"We'll just play it by ear," Autumn said stiffly.

"Thank you for understanding," Tuckered muttered distractedly, his fingers tapping the steering wheel in a nervous rhythm.

Her understanding? If he only knew how wrong he was. Despite Tucker's reassurance otherwise, something, no make that someone, had gotten him all out of sorts. She doubted it was one of his brothers. She felt confident Tucker would have told her so. The sheriff? She didn't think so. This was someone he preferred not to make mention of by name. Her troubled thoughts began to stir. Could his caller have been a woman? Tucker had never said anything about being in a relationship with anyone, but it stood to reason that a man as handsome and as personable as Tucker Wade would have plenty of women vying for his attention.

If Tucker were seeing someone, then it only made sense that whomever she was would feel understandably neglected. Tucker had spent all his free time with Autumn and his daughter since their arrival there. More troublesome was the possibility that if there was a woman in Tucker's life, one who had the ability to make him drop everything, plans with his daughter included, to run to her in all haste, Autumn was going to have to reevaluate Tucker's commitment to his daughter.

Tucker made no further attempt to explain his being called away. In fact, he drove in silence the rest of the trip back to his place. If not for Blue singing silly little made-up songs about horses and chickens and kitties, the drive would have been beyond uncomfortable.

When Tucker pulled up in front of his ranch house, Autumn was more than ready to get out of his truck. "Stay there," she told him. "You're in a hurry. I'll see to Blue." She didn't wait for his assistance before jumping down from the truck's cab and getting her niece out of the car seat.

"We'll talk when I get back," he called after her.

"If you can spare the time," she cast back over her shoulder as she led Blue away toward the house, unable to look back as Tucker drove away.

"Are you mad at Daddy?" Blue asked as they made their way inside the cedar-sided ranch house.

Autumn forced a smile. "No, honey. Just a little disappointed that we couldn't finish our tour." And a lot disappointed in your daddy, she struggled not to add. Blue had to come first to whomever she ended up with. If Tucker weren't willing to do so, then Autumn most certainly would.

"I'm hungry."

"Let's go see what we can throw together for dinner," she told her niece.

"Can I have a grilled cheese?" Blue asked.

Autumn smiled. "I think I can manage that."

They made their way into the kitchen where her niece settled herself onto one of the kitchen chairs. "Daddy likes grilled cheese."

As far as she was concerned, Tucker could fend for himself. "It would be cold before your daddy gets home."

Whenever that would be. And what would Tucker have done if she hadn't been there to leave Blue with? Drop her off with one of his brothers? His parents? That was not what she considered taking on responsibility.

A short while later, a knock sounded at the front door. Before Autumn could go answer it, the door cracked open. "Tucker?"

"Jackson?" she called out as she stepped from the kitchen.

"Did the nursing home get ahold of my brother?" he asked as he moved toward her with that slightly off-kilter gait of his. He looked every bit as troubled as Tucker had been after he'd made his phone call.

"Nursing home?"

"Apparently, Old Wylie is having a bad spell. They've been trying to reach my brother for over an hour with no luck. I told them I would see if I could find him."

"Uncle Jackson!" Blue exclaimed from the kitchen doorway, a half-eaten grilled cheese sandwich pinched between her fingers.

A wide grin spread across his face at the sight of her. "Hey there, kiddo."

"Did you come for a grilled cheese sandwich?"

"Not today," he told her. "I have an errand to run."

"Sweetie," Autumn said, "go back to the table to finish your sandwich. I'll be in as soon as I'm done talking to your uncle Jackson."

"Okay," she said, taking a bite of her sandwich and then added around a mouthful of cheese and bread, "Bye, Uncle Jackson."

"Bye, cutie-pie."

She smiled at the affectionate nickname her uncle had given her and then disappeared back into the kitchen.

All of the anger that had been building up inside Autumn toward Tucker after he'd left without any real explanation was immediately replaced by guilt as she turned back to his brother. "I take it Old Wylie is a relative of yours?"

Tucker's brother shook his head. "No. He's an old rodeo rider who took Tucker under his wing when my brother was first starting out, teaching him the ins and outs of bronc riding. Unfortunately, Old Wylie has been having bouts of dementia and sometimes he has these panic attacks. Tucker's the only one who seems to be able to calm him down."

Autumn put a hand to her mouth. She felt ill. She'd judged Tucker so badly. So wrongly.

"Autumn?" Jackson said, his worried frown deepening. "You okay?"

"Yes," she said with a nod. "I just know how frightening it can be for an older person when they are feeling panicked or confused. My grandmother…" She didn't finish her explanation. Instead, she said, "Tucker is already on his way to the nursing home."

That announcement didn't appear to relieve Jackson at all. "I'd best get going. He'll need Hank." No doubt seeing the confusion on her face, he added, "His guitar. He left it in the back of my truck."

Tucker played guitar, she thought in surprise. Confused, she asked, "What does his guitar have to do with your brother being called to the nursing home?"

"A great deal," he replied. "My brother goes to the home a couple of times a month—that is when we're not on the road with the rodeo—to sing and play for Old Wylie and the other residents there."

"Your brother sings?" Summer had never made mention of it. And since arriving at Bent Creek she'd never even heard Tucker so much as hum a tune.

Jackson nodded. "He does. But most people don't know about his musical ability. He never played or sang around anyone other than family until he started doing it at Sunny Days. Old Wylie is a fan of old-time camp-fire songs, so Tucker took his guitar in one time to indulge the old man. His playing and singing there ended up becoming a regular thing for all of the residents."

"That's so sweet of him," Autumn said, Tucker's kindness touching her deeply.

"Don't tell him that," Jackson said with a grin. "We cowboys don't like to be thought of as sweet. Makes us sound soft."

Autumn laughed. "You are soft. All of you Wade brothers. I've seen you around my niece. Marshmallows have nothing on you three."

He chuckled in response. "You might be right. At least when it comes to Blue. I should get going. I need to get Hank to Tucker. Hopefully, my brother will be able to calm Old Wylie down." He started back out the door.

"Jackson…"

He paused to look back at her.

"Would you mind if I took Hank to Tucker?"

He shrugged. "I suppose I could stay here and keep an eye on Blue while you run Tucker's guitar to him."

"No need," she said with a grateful smile. "I'll take her with me."

His brows creased. "Are you sure? Some of the residents there are not in the best shape. It might be upsetting for her."

"I'm sure," she told him with a smile, grateful that her niece's well-being was foremost in his mind. "Blue and I occasionally pay visits to nursing homes back in Cheyenne. Your niece loves to hand out pages she's colored to the residents. Not as much as she loves sitting with them and spinning all sorts of tales that keep her aging audience quite entertained." Her smile softened. "I suppose she's a lot like her daddy in that way."

"I suppose it's true what they say then. The apple doesn't fall far from the tree," he agreed.

She hoped not. The last thing she wanted to be was anything at all like her own parents had been. Autumn turned, calling out to Blue. "Blue, sweetie, go get your boots and coat on. We're going for a ride." Then she looked back to Jackson. "You can give me directions to Sunny Days while I walk out with you to get Hank."

With a nod, he followed her outside.

When they arrived at the nursing home less than ten minutes later, Autumn reached for Blue's hand, Tucker's guitar held securely in her other hand. The sound of masculine singing filtered through the hallway, growing louder as they neared the recreation room.

"I can hear him," Blue said in an excited whisper, having learned that quiet voices were best for places like this.

Autumn could, as well. Tucker had a beautiful voice, not that she would ever word it that way to him. She was learning that men of his breed liked to think themselves manly men. The thought made her smile. Those three hulking, ex-rodeo riding brothers couldn't get any manlier if they tried. She gave Blue's hand a gentle squeeze. "I'm not so sure he even needs Hank." They slowed, turning to step through the open doorway.

The oversized, window-lined room was filled with what were clearly Tucker Wade's adoring fans. Seated on settees and chairs, and a few scattered wheelchairs, the residents were undeniably enthralled by Tucker's melodic voice. Despite not having his trusty guitar to accompany him, he was singing his heart out, his grin aimed at one particular resident seated in the front row. The older man, despite his frail appearance, was clapping his hands and tapping a foot to Tucker's deep baritone voice singing "Back in the Saddle Again."

Standing there, watching Tucker bring joy to so many faces with his singing made Autumn's heart melt. There had been no singing cowboy during her grandma's final days, which had been spent in a nursing home very similar to the one she was standing in now. Her grandma would have enjoyed it so very much. Tucker Wade was turning out to be the most giving man she had ever known. She sniffed softly, her eyes misting over.

"Aunt Autumn, why are you crying?" Blue asked, forgetting to use her quiet voice, causing several heads to turn in their direction.

The shifting commotion at the back of the room drew Tucker's gaze in her and Blue's direction. The second he saw them standing there, his green eyes widened in surprise, the song he'd been singing coming to a jarring halt.

The abrupt end to the song had the home's residents stirring anxiously. Pleas for him to finish his song filled the room. Tucker shifted uneasily, a hint of color deepening his tanned cheeks.

Autumn hadn't meant to embarrass him. Truth was she wasn't even sure why she had volunteered to bring his guitar to him instead of letting his brother see to the task. But she'd judged him so unfairly. She'd wanted to make it up to him. Leaning down, she said to Blue, "We know the song your daddy was singing. How about we sing along with him?" Having seen her fair share of old Westerns, she knew plenty of cowboy campfire songs, many of which she had taught Blue to sing.

Blue nodded eagerly at the suggestion.

Lifting her gaze to Tucker, who stood watching her from across the room, Autumn began to sing. Blue quickly joined in and the two of them made their way through the gathered residents, their smiles returning once more. As they drew closer to Tucker, she held Hank out to him with a warm smile. "We thought you might be needing this," she whispered as Blue continued singing at the top of her precious little lungs.

With a nod of appreciation, he took the guitar and eased its strap over his head. Feeding his muscular arm through the loop, he let the weight of the instrument fall against his jean-clad hip as he began to play. Then his deep, baritone voice joined hers and Blue's, blending perfectly, as together they finished the remainder of the song.

After playing several more well-known songs, his singing accompanied by that of his daughter and her beautiful aunt, the home's staff began to escort the residents from the room for their evening meal. But Old Wylie was far too smitten with Autumn to concern himself with nourishment. Once introductions had been made, the older man had been more than content to chatter on, all cow eyed, with Autumn.

Tucker's gaze was drawn to Autumn's smiling face. She didn't appear to mind the older man's determination to chew her ear off. Instead, she sat grinning, laughing at Wylie's stories even if they verged on being what Tucker would consider very tall tales.

He turned his attention to Blue, who was seated at a table by the window, putting a puzzle together with one of the home's good-hearted volunteers. She never ceased to amaze him. At times, even humble him. When he'd first seen her standing just inside the recreation room's open doorway with Autumn, he'd pretty much been stunned speechless. Or songless as was the case.

When Autumn's pale blue gaze had met his, he'd not missed the sheen of unshed tears in her eyes. His first thought had been to sweep Blue out of the room, away from what was sure to upset her or at the very least, make his daughter uneasy. But Blue hadn't balked one bit at being surrounded by a roomful of elderly patients, some of whom were hooked up to oxygen, some in wheelchairs, even those like Old Wylie, who suffered from various levels of dementia. She had fallen into song, right alongside her beautiful aunt, making Tucker forget all about wanting to sweep her from the room. Instead, he'd waited where he'd been standing for them to reach him, moved by their sweet voices.

As if sensing his gaze upon her, Blue glanced up from the puzzle she was working on, and a happy smile stretched across her tiny heart-shaped face. A face he prayed he would spend the rest of his life being able to look upon.

Wylie's attendant returned to take him to supper, having allowed the older man extra time with Tucker and his guests. With a word of thanks to Tucker, she escorted her now much-calmer patient from the room.

When they had gone, Autumn turned to him. "Why didn't you tell us you were coming here?"

A slight frown pinched at his lips. "I didn't want to

bring up sad memories for you, your having had to care for your ailing grandmother and all."

Her expression softened. "I wish you would have. Seeing you here…" Emotion had the words catching in her throat. "Well, it was just so kindhearted of you. If I had known—"

He cut her off, saying, "I don't do this for the praise. God gave me the ability to play, so why not use it to make others happy?"

"You might not seek praise, but you most certainly deserve it. And I agree, the good Lord definitely blessed you with the ability to play *and* sing. You have a wonderful voice."

"If we're talking being blessed with the ability to sing, I'd have to say that *He* gifted you, as well."

Her cheeks pinkened. "Thank you."

He gave a slight nod. Truth was, Autumn had truly surprised him with her genuine ease around the home's residents. But his daughter had surprised him even more. "I can't get over how easily Blue adapted to things here."

She glanced toward his daughter, her smile softening even more. "Blue is a very bighearted little girl. And this isn't the first nursing home she's been to."

His brows drew together in confusion. "But I thought your grandmother passed away years ago."

"She did," she said, a hint of sadness lacing her voice. "But there are so many other elderly people spending their final days in homes like this who have no family to look in on them." Autumn went on to explain how she and Blue paid visits to different nursing homes back in Cheyenne with the hopes of brightening the residents' days, just as Autumn had once done for her grandmother before her passing.

"Thank you for teaching my daughter to treat others with patience and kindness."

"Tucker…"

"Yes?"

"Do you think it would be all right if Blue and I come back with you next time you play for the patients? If we're still here, I mean," she added. "Just to watch."

"I'd like that," he said. "In fact, you and Blue can join me in entertaining the residents."

She shook her head. "Oh, we couldn't do that. It's your special time with them."

"You and Blue made it even more special. And I know the residents really enjoyed having the two of you here." He reached out, placing his hand atop hers. "So did I."

"I'm glad we came," she said softly. "It gave me a chance to see yet another side of the man you are. Beyond the strong, loyal, loving brother, son and father you have shown yourself to be. You're compassionate to others and a truly devoted friend. A very likable man. I can see why my sister was drawn to you."

And you? he wanted to ask, but kept those words to himself. Withdrawing his hand, despite the urge to leave it exactly where it was, he said, "Well, you're pretty likable, too."

"Thank you." She glanced in his daughter's direction. "We should be going."

"I won't be long behind you. I just want to stop by the cafeteria and make sure Wylie is still doing okay."

She stood and looked down at him with a tender smile. "Do what you need to do. Blue and I will see you when you get home."

He watched as she crossed the room to collect Blue, his heart giving odd little lurches. Could he really let

Autumn go back to Cheyenne without telling her how he felt? Feelings he was still trying to work out. Because he'd opened his heart to a woman once before and had ended up being left to pick up the pieces after Summer had trampled over it. Did he dare risk it a second time?

Chapter Nine

"For years, I've been surrounded by men," Emma Wade said as she and Autumn peeled potatoes for that night's family dinner. "It's so nice to finally have another female around." Her gaze slid over to Blue whose job was to place the peeled potatoes, once they had been rinsed, into a bowl that sat on the table in front of her and then hand them to her grandma to cut into pieces. A tender smile moved over Emma's face as she corrected her previous statement. "Two females, counting Blue."

"It was kind of you to include me in tonight's dinner," Autumn told her as she walked over to the sink to rinse off another colander full of potatoes.

"You're family, honey," the older woman replied as she sliced into a wedge of potato. "Of course, you're invited to join us."

There it was again, being told that she was part of a family that had no real familial connection with her. At least, not directly. It would have been nice to truly be a part of this family. They were everything Autumn had wished for growing up, but had never had. Loving, giving, warmhearted and unfailingly loyal.

"Aunt Autumn's gonna come live with us."

The colander Autumn was holding under the water's stream clattered into the kitchen sink as it slipped from her grasp. She cast a glance back over her shoulder to find Tucker's momma staring at her wide-eyed.

"You are?"

Autumn gave an embarrassed laugh as she retrieved the potato-laden colander, which had thankfully remained upright when it slipped from her hands. "I think Blue would like that to be true. However, I do have an open invitation to come visit anytime I like if Blue comes to live here in Bent Creek with her daddy."

"Of course, you do," the older woman replied as she went back to dicing another potato. "I'm just sorry you've been put in such an emotionally draining situation. I hope Tucker's been sensitive of the position you're in."

Tucker, she thought with an odd ache in her heart. He was everything she wanted in a man. But he was not the man for her. Because if she gave in to her feelings and Tucker reciprocated she would spend the rest of her life knowing she was once again another man's second choice.

"It hasn't been easy for him, either," Autumn replied, "but we're working our way through it. Tucker has been incredibly understanding about my need to make certain I do what I feel is in Blue's best interest."

"Glad to hear it," his momma said. "I'd expect no less from any of my boys."

"Your son...all of your sons," she corrected, "are fine men who could give the gentlemen of Texas a run for their money in the manners department."

Pride lit the older woman's face. "Well, you be sure

to tell me if any of them have a lapse of manners and I'll set them straight."

Autumn laughed softly. "I'll do that." Not that she truly believed that would ever happen. Their manners were too deeply ingrained. And although Blue was too young to fully appreciate what she had gained by this trip, Autumn knew. Her niece now had a complete family on her daddy's side, all of whom wanted to make her a part of their lives. Family who would love and cherish her as she so deserved to be.

While she was so incredibly happy for Blue, to have been so easily accepted and loved without reservation, she had to admit, at least to herself, that a part of her envied her young niece. She immediately pushed the thought away, because envy had no place in her life, and busied herself with rinsing off the next batch of potatoes while Emma and Blue chatted away behind her.

The kitchen door swung open, and Garrett poked his head inside. "Afternoon," he greeted, immediately sweeping the black cowboy hat from his head.

"You're early," his momma said in surprise.

"My last appointment canceled," he answered as he stepped inside. "Figured I'd come over as soon as I had washed up." His gaze swept the kitchen. "Where's Tucker?"

"Jackson called to say an old tree uprooted between your place and his and was lying halfway across the road. Your father and Tucker went out to help him clear it away."

"Well, I had a surprise I wanted to show Blue, but I suppose it can wait. I'd best go lend them a hand."

Blue looked to Autumn in silent pleading. "But I like surprises."

"Honey," his mother said, clicking her tongue. "You can't dangle a carrot in front of a rabbit and then take it away like that."

Confusion lit Garrett's face.

Autumn fought to keep her smile from widening. The Wade brothers were mostly clueless when it came to children, but adorably so.

"You have a rabbit?" Blue asked excitedly.

"I...um..."

"No, sweetie," Autumn answered for Garrett, who appeared to be momentarily tongue-tied. "It's just a saying."

Relief swept over Garrett's features. "Maybe so, but in this case I really do have a rabbit."

Blue gasped. "You do?"

His smile widened. "I do. Its mother belongs to a customer of mine's little boy. Her baby needed a little extra care after he was born, so I've been watching over him and seeing to it that he gets the care he needs until he's ready to go back to his family."

Blue looked worried. "Will he be okay?"

"Better than okay," Tucker's brother assured her. "In fact, I'm taking him back to his mother after dinner this evening, but I thought you might like to have a peek at him. Maybe even pet him if you'd like to."

"I'd like to!" Blue said excitedly. "Are we gonna go to your pet store to see him?"

Garrett's husky chuckle sounded a lot like Tucker's, maybe slightly deeper. "I don't mean to disappoint you, honey, but I don't have a pet store. Just a small building that sits next to my house that I sometimes use to care for animals. However, we don't have to go anywhere." He thumbed back over his shoulder toward the door he'd just come through. "I have Mr. Cottontail out on the back porch in a special cage that will keep him safe from other animals and warm."

"Can I go see him?" Blue asked, turning pleading green eyes to Autumn.

"Maybe after we finish helping your grandma with the potatoes," she told her.

"Oh, I think you and I can handle the rest of these without Blue's help," Tucker's momma said. "Don't you?"

If she didn't mind, Autumn didn't, either. Blue had been happier these past couple of weeks than she had been in months. "I reckon we can manage," she agreed with a tender smile aimed in her niece's direction.

Blue jumped down from the table and started toward the door where her uncle waited.

"Hold on, sweetie," Autumn said. "You need your jacket."

"I've got it," Garrett said, lifting the tiny coat from the hook that held it on the rack beside where he stood at the door. Then he knelt to help her into it. "All set," he said, rising to his feet.

Autumn hurried over to zip her niece's weighted jacket. "It's a little chilly out," she told her with a loving smile.

"Okay," Garrett said, "let's go see that bunny."

With a squeal, Blue was out the door in a flash. He glanced back at Autumn with a grin. "A girl right after her uncle's heart." Shoving his hat back onto his head, he followed Blue out onto the porch, swinging the door shut behind him.

As soon as the door closed, Emma Wade shook her head. "That boy of mine, always going over and above to help those with animals in need. He's a large animal vet. How on God's green earth does a rabbit fit into that category?"

That made Autumn smile. "He has a good heart."

"One he should be using to find someone special," she muttered as she began cleaning up the peelings they'd left behind on the table. She looked up at Autumn. "How is he ever going to meet the right woman when he spends all of his time caring for animals? How are any of my boys going to find their other half for that matter? All they think about is horses and rodeos."

Autumn understood the root of Emma's frustration. She wanted her sons to be happy, and to her that meant finding someone to love. It was clear, just being around Tucker's parents for even a short time that they were very happy in their marriage. "How did you and Grady meet?" she asked as she gathered up their dirty paring knives.

Emma's expression softened. "We met at the Spring County Fair Rodeo. He had just gotten bucked off a bronc right in front of the bleacher seats my family and I were seated in. When he stood, our eyes met." The older woman's wistful smile widened. "It was as if his boots had taken root right there in that very spot, because he just stood there grinning up at me. They practically had to drag him from the arena. When the rodeo let out, Grady was waiting for us at the exit. He asked my father right then and there for permission to take me out."

"He didn't even ask if you had anyone special in your life first?"

Emma laughed. "Oh, no. Grady said the good Lord had him tossed onto his backside in that very spot for a reason—to meet his future wife."

"I take it your daddy said yes," Autumn said, thoroughly caught up in Emma's love story.

"My father said that Grady was welcome to join us for early church service the next morning. I think my father expected Grady not to show. But he did, greeting me that morning in his Sunday best, with that deep-dimpled smile. I nearly melted."

"Love at first sight," Autumn said with a sigh.

"We were definitely taken with each other," Tucker's momma said. "But the love came later, growing day by day as we got to know each other. And you know the rest."

"So you married a man whose life once centered around the rodeo and ended up happily married with three wonderful sons," Autumn replied. "Sons who hold the same passion for the rodeo as their father. I think you need to have faith. When love is meant to happen for your boys, for anyone, it will." She had to believe that. Because, unlike her own momma, Autumn truly did long to have a family of her very own. One she could share stories with, laugh with, go to church with, even have family dinners with. All the things she'd never gotten the chance to experience growing up.

Emma set the dish towel she'd been wiping the table with down and turned to Autumn. "How can someone so young be so wise?"

Warmth crept into Autumn's cheeks. "I don't know about being wise. I'm just a hopeless romantic." *Hopeless* being the key word in her case when it came to finding love. She had to wonder if she would even know what true love was if it ever did come her way. A love like Emma had found with Grady.

Booted footsteps sounded in the hallway. A moment later, Tucker came to a stop in the kitchen doorway, a dimpled grin stretched wide across his handsome face. When his gaze met hers, Autumn's heart gave an unexpected kick.

"You're back sooner than I expected," his momma said.

"It was a small tree," he answered with a shrug of his broad shoulders as he stepped farther into the room. "Barely more than a twig."

"In other words," Autumn said, trying to suppress a smile as she moved past him to dry off the table Tucker's momma had just wiped down, "you left us here to do the hard work of peeling all of those potatoes while you and your daddy went off to push a few twigs off the road..."

Tucker's brow lifted in an exaggerated affront. "Are you calling me a shirker?"

Autumn laughed. "If the shoe fits..."

"If you two will excuse me," Tucker's momma said with a barely suppressed smile. "I think I'll go outside and have a peek at that baby bunny Garrett brought to show Blue." Without waiting for their response, his momma slipped out the back door, closing it quickly behind her.

Tucker groaned, drawing Autumn's gaze his way. "Is something wrong?"

"Tell me we're not taking the bunny home to live with us. I'm not so sure Itty Bitty would appreciate having to share her new home with a pet rabbit."

Autumn shook her head. "You're off the hook. The bunny isn't for Blue. Your brother has been tending to it and wanted Blue to see it before he takes it back to its owner tonight."

He exhaled a huge sigh. "Well, that's a relief. I had

visions of my brother gifting Blue with a fluffy little lamb next."

"He'd better not," Autumn said, cringing at the thought. "I don't know anything about taking care of farm animals. I'm almost in over my head with a kitten."

"Oh, I don't know. I'd say you've adapted pretty well," he told her with that devastating Wade grin she'd become so fond of. "A good thing since I doubt my daughter is going to want to leave Bitty behind when the two of you go back to Cheyenne."

Autumn's smile sagged, despite the effort she made to hide her emotions. Tucker had no way of knowing she'd made her decision, the hardest she'd ever had to make. Blue belonged with her daddy. Only now she wouldn't just be leaving her niece in Bent Creek, she feared she'd be leaving a piece of her heart, as well. She prayed Summer would forgive her for falling for Tucker, something she'd never expected to happen. Not in a million years. But having seen him with Blue, with his family, with Old Wylie, how could she not?

"Autumn?"

She met Tucker's searching gaze.

"You okay?" he asked, concern etched in his features.

She mentally shoved her woes aside. There would be time enough later, when she was alone, to dwell on such things. "It's just that I've been so caught up in getting to know you and your family that sometimes I forget my time here is coming to an end."

"Speaking of time," Tucker said as he moved to stand in front of her. Taking the dish towel from Autumn's hand, he placed it on the table. "We've got some to spare before dinner is ready. What do you say we pick up our ranch tour where we left off the other day?"

She looked around, making sure the mess they had made while preparing the potatoes was all cleaned up. "Your momma has the roast in the oven and the potatoes are ready to boil. I suppose my job here is done." Her gaze shifted back to Tucker. "I'll go fetch Blue."

"Good luck getting her away from the bunny," he told her.

"Probably true," she agreed. And it would give her a chance to talk to Tucker about turning custody of Blue over to him. Just the thought of it had a lump of emotion forming in her throat. "But your momma is busy with dinner preparations. I don't feel right asking her to keep an eye on Blue, too."

His dimpled grin returned. "Blue is her granddaughter. I'm pretty sure my mom, my whole family in fact, would be more than happy to watch over her anytime we need them to."

"We'll ask them just to be sure," Autumn said as she reached for her coat.

"I'm good with that. Here, let me," Tucker said, reaching past her to lift the coat from its hook.

"Always the gentleman," she teased as she slid her arm into the sleeve he was holding up for her.

"I try my best," he replied with a grin as he held up the other sleeve.

"I don't think there's much trying involved," she said, glancing back over her shoulder at him. "Your momma taught her sons well."

"She did her best," he said as he settled the coat onto her shoulders. "I'm sure we didn't make it easy for her."

Autumn turned with a smile. "Real handfuls, were you?"

"You could say that," he said as he reached out to pull

the front of her coat together. "Unfortunately for Mom," he continued, surprising her as he latched the zipper together and eased it carefully upward, "my brothers and I inherited a good portion of Dad's wild streak. But there's no denying that it came in handy during our rodeo days."

"How so?" she asked, trying to recall the last time someone had done something so thoughtful for her.

"A man has to have a little bit of wildness in him to climb onto a two-thousand-pound bull, or to mount a horse whose natural inclination is to buck and buck hard," he replied, giving her coat's zipper one final, gentle tug before releasing it.

"W-was it the same for barrel racers?" Autumn asked, trying not to focus on the small act of kindness that Tucker had just shown her. "Because Summer..." her words trailed off, her regretful gaze lifting to meet Tucker's. "I'm sorry. I shouldn't have brought my sister up after everything that's happened."

"She did me wrong," he said. "No doubt about it. But she was still your sister and Blue's mother. I don't want either of you to feel like you can't talk about her. And, to answer your question, yes, Summer definitely had a wild streak of her own. Her not being afraid to take risks helped make her one of the best barrel racers in the business when she competed."

Autumn turned back to where her purse hung from another hook on the coatrack and reached inside it to retrieve her cell phone. Sliding it into the front pocket of her coat, she said, "I should've taken time to go watch her compete in rodeos, but I was so busy trying to get my real estate business off the ground."

His smile softened as he reached for the door. "I'm sure your sister understood. You were both just trying to follow your hearts." Opening the door, he said, "And speaking of hearts, let's go see if my family minds watching over the little girl who has completely captured mine."

His wasn't the only heart that Blue had captured, Autumn thought with a sad smile as they stepped out onto the porch. Because she had finally accepted that Blue belonged there with Tucker and his warm, loving family. It wasn't what she wanted, but it was what her niece deserved, and Autumn would never deny her that. It was time to prepare herself for letting Blue go.

Tucker walked Autumn out to his truck. Then he settled himself behind the steering wheel. "My mother really likes having you around."

"I enjoy being around her," Autumn replied. "Around your whole family, for that matter."

They pulled away from the ranch house and then turned onto the road that cut across his family's land. "I don't think they could like you any more if they tried," Tucker told her. Himself included. Especially after she'd brought his guitar to him at the nursing home. That day he'd seen more than just her beautiful, smiling face and deep-rooted love for his daughter. He'd seen her put herself out there to sing for the home's residents, quite beautifully at that. He'd watched her kindhearted interaction with those around her, making each and every one of their elderly audience feel special. But it was her tender compassion and patience when it came to Old Wylie that had managed to whittle away the last protective layer he'd kept around his heart since Summer had walked out on him. Lord help him but he was falling for Autumn and falling hard.

"Are those yours?"

Drawn from his thoughts, Tucker followed the line of Autumn's gaze to the herd of broncs moving across the distant pasture. Their lean muscular forms moved together in a majestic grace that seemed so at odds with the wild, bucking creatures they became the second they left the chute and entered the rodeo arena.

Tucker smiled. "Mine and my brothers'. Would you like to have a closer look at them?"

She glanced his way, excitement lighting her eyes. "Very much so."

"There's a gate just up the road," he told her. "We'll go in there."

Autumn couldn't seem to take her eyes off the horses. *A good thing*, Tucker thought. Because he couldn't seem to keep his eyes off her.

"You've mentioned selling your real estate business in Texas to move up here to Wyoming to help Summer out," Tucker said, needing to redirect his thoughts.

She gave a slight nod. "I did."

"Do you ever regret it?"

Autumn took a long moment to mull the question over. "I can't say that I do. I thought about it long and hard before making the change. Summer would never have asked me to. She would have continued to try to handle things on her own. But my sister's pride wouldn't have guaranteed a roof over their heads, or food on the table. So I made the decision for them."

"I'm grateful you did."

"No, I'm the one who's grateful. It allowed me to spend precious time with my sister that I might not have had if I had chosen my business over helping Summer out during her time of need."

Autumn had to be the most selfless person he'd ever known. Blue was blessed to have such a loving aunt in her life. "I'm thankful you were there for them. I'm just sorry you had to give up something that meant so much to you."

"I'm still able to do what I love," she added with a soft smile. "I just work for someone else now."

He had to admire her outlook on things. He wasn't so certain he'd be as accepting of them if he were in her position. It had to be hard going from running your own business to answering to someone else.

"So how does this rodeo contracting thing work?" Autumn asked as they drove down the road.

Pleased by her interest in something he was passionate about, Tucker went on to explain the most important aspects of his business from contracting with rodeos to transporting the horses to the events. Then he gave her a quick rundown on how things worked once the rodeos began.

"That's quite a demanding schedule," Autumn remarked.

He shrugged. "It's not so bad. Our working hours depend on a multitude of things, the season, changing weather conditions, foaling time and whether or not we are in the midst of rodeo commitments. You and Blue couldn't have come at a better time," he told her. "It's October, which means rodeo season has ended and our bucking horses are enjoying some free time to do their own thing. Same goes for my brothers and I for the most part."

When they reached the gate that he'd told Autumn about, Tucker turned off the road and put the truck in Park. "I'll be right back." Jumping out, he hurried around to open the heavy metal gate. Then he slid back in behind the wheel and pulled through the opening. "Give me a sec to close the gate and then we'll get going."

"There are so many horses," Autumn said as she watched them through the window.

"The Triple W has one of the largest selections of broncs, which includes some of the most sought-after rodeo broncs around."

"They're magnificent."

Tucker's chest puffed with pride. "We tend to think so. Even of the retired ones."

She looked at him questioningly.

"When our broncs have done their time in the rodeo, we put them in an area we've fenced off especially for retirement stock. They can roam at leisure and enjoy their final years."

Autumn looked back out over the expanse of land before them and the herd that was now traversing one of the rocky hillsides. "They're very blessed to have found a home here."

"I hope you'll feel the same way about Blue coming to live here," he said. "Everything you see is a part of her heritage, her future. She'll be able to travel with me during rodeo season and learn the ins and outs of the family business from a young age."

"Travel with you to rodeos?" Autumn repeated, her expression changing.

"Only if she chooses to," he hurried to add. "If she's not comfortable with it, she can stay here."

"Stay here with who?" she asked, her words sounding more clipped.

"Her grandparents," he said, questioning his own reply even as it left his mouth.

Autumn sat back, her expression pained. "This isn't gonna work."

Tucker's brows drew together in confusion. "What isn't going to work?"

"Blue's staying here," she said, taking him by surprise. "I was prepared to let her go, to leave her here with you when I went back to Cheyenne. But, after this talk, I realize it wouldn't be in Blue's best interest."

Tucker struggled to form a response to her announcement. "I don't understand. What did I do to make you feel Blue shouldn't be with me?"

"Let me verify something. Will you be gone for months with your rodeo business? Or will someone be going in your place for even part of that time?"

"We've had this discussion before. I'll be away for at least a month of that time. Maybe longer. It depends on our schedule. But my parents are more than willing to keep Blue for me while I'm away."

"Blue's emotional security is more important than any schedule. And while you have so many wonderful qualities to offer a child, the truth is your life isn't conducive to raising one. Not with all the traveling you have to do when rodeo season rolls around. That being the case, I don't feel comfortable leaving Blue here to be, at times, shuffled around and left feeling as if she'd been abandoned by her daddy."

All Tucker could focus on was Autumn's sudden change of heart where custody of Blue was concerned. Or was it all that sudden? Had this been her plan all along? To make him think she was giving him a chance when she really had no intention of turning Blue over to him. Maybe she wasn't so different from her sister after all. Just as his wife had done, Autumn was going to take his daughter away from him. And to think he'd nearly made a fool of himself by telling Autumn how he truly felt about her.

"I've done everything you've asked of me to convince you my daughter belongs here with me, but it's not enough. Would it ever have been enough?" he demanded. "Because you knew what I did for a living before you showed up on my doorstep that day. Yet, here you are using my rodeo business against me."

Tears filled her eyes. "Yes, I knew what you did. But I thought things might change once you realized you had responsibilities toward Blue. And while I adore your momma, your leaving Blue for days, even weeks on end to be cared for by her is not much different than what my momma did to us, leaving care of Summer and I to our grandma."

"I'm not your mother or your father," he growled in frustration. "And I'd appreciate your not comparing me to them." Swiping his cowboy hat from his head, Tucker dragged a hand back through his hair. What frustrated him the most was her not being able to see that unlike her parents he would do everything in his power to see to his daughter's happiness. Even if he had to be away for short periods of time. That meant he loved Blue no less. Taking stock to the rodeos was his livelihood.

"I think we should head back now," Autumn said with a sniffle.

He looked at her and even now, after her telling him she would be taking his daughter away from him, he still felt the urge to brush the trail of hot, salty tears from her cheeks. Fool he was.

"Agreed," Tucker replied. "I've got more meaningful things I could be doing right now, like spending time with my daughter before you take her away. Speaking of which, do you intend to let me tell Blue goodbye when the time comes, or will you just slip away with her like Summer did all those years ago?"

She gasped at his harsh words, and Tucker knew immediate regret at having spoken them. "Unlike my sister," she said, her words choked with emotion, "I would never do that to you. But I suggest you say your goodbyes to Blue tonight, because we'll be leaving for Cheyenne first thing tomorrow morning."

"Tucker," Garrett called after him as Tucker crossed his parents' yard to his truck.

Stopping, he turned to find not only Garrett, but Jackson striding his way, concern written all over their faces.

"The barn," his oldest brother said as he moved right on past him. "Now."

He looked to Jackson who only shook his head as he followed Garrett.

Tucker wasn't up for this. Whatever "this" was going to be. Sitting there at dinner, knowing what Autumn planned to do, had filled him with hurt and anger, and a whole lot of frustration. But he fell into step behind his brothers.

Garrett closed the barn door behind them, guaranteeing privacy. Then he turned back to Tucker. "Let's talk."

Tucker's frown deepened as his brothers stood pinning him with their stares, arms folded unbudgingly across their flannel-covered chests. Dinner at his parents' place that evening had been strained. At least, where he and Autumn were concerned. Not that she'd made any mention of their disagreement to his family. She'd been polite to everyone, smiling when the conver-

sation required it and acting as if she hadn't just trampled all over his trust. More tellingly, he supposed, was
the fact that Autumn had avoided meeting his gaze as
they sat across the table from each other, directing her
conversation to everyone but him.

Exhaling deeply, Tucker muttered, "Autumn and I
had words."

Jackson snorted. "I don't think either of us would
have to be professional investigators to have figured
that one out."

Tucker shot him a warning glance. "This is no joke.
It's my daughter Autumn intends to take away from me."

Jackson threw up a hand. "Wait a minute. What?"

"She's taking Blue home," he said, his voice breaking. "She's going to fight me for custody."

Surprise registered on Garrett's face. "Why?"

"I thought the two of you were working everything
out," Jackson said.

He nodded. "We were. Unfortunately, Autumn has
had a change of heart where my rodeo travel time as
part-owner of the Triple W comes into play."

"Unless I missed something," Garrett said, "Autumn
knew what you did for a living when she came here to
see what kind of father you would be to Blue. Why is
she having issues with it now?"

"There's so much more to it than my being away at
times," he said, turning to face them as he filled his
brothers in on a bit more of Autumn's background and
how she had essentially lumped him right in with her
parents when he'd mentioned that his mom and dad
would watch over Blue on occasion when he had to
travel for work.

"That explains the weird tension between you and Autumn at dinner tonight," Jackson said.

"I didn't do anything wrong," Tucker said in his own defense.

"We know that," Garrett said. "And I'm pretty sure Autumn does, too. But her past feeds into her protective instincts where Blue's concerned."

"I'm not Autumn's parents," Tucker ground out. "My leaving Blue with Mom and Dad isn't abandoning my daughter."

"Maybe not," Jackson acknowledged. "But think about it, Tucker. How would you feel if the proverbial shoe was on the other foot? What if you gave up custody to Autumn and she left Blue in someone else's care while she went out of town for her job for extended periods of time?"

He'd been so hurt by Autumn's unfair condemnation of him that he hadn't allowed himself to appreciate the true depth of her concern. Shame for the way he had handled his end of their conversation filled him. How would he feel if the roles were reversed and he was going to place his daughter in the hands of someone who wouldn't personally be around to see to Blue's care for days, even weeks on end?

Tucker yanked off his hat and dragged a hand back through his hair. Then he looked up at his brothers. "I would've done the same thing."

"There you have it," Garrett said. "So what are you willing to do to keep you daughter in your life?"

Hadn't he already done everything in his power to prove to Autumn that Blue belonged with him? Everything, apparently, except give up his part of a business he'd built from the ground up alongside his brothers. A business he took immense pride in. But that pride had never been felt as deep as the love he had for his little girl. A business didn't greet you with open arms when you came home at the end of the day. It didn't make you see flowers and butterflies, even family dinners in a whole new light. It didn't love you unconditionally.

Slapping his hat back onto his head, Tucker stepped past his brothers and pushed open the barn door.

"Where are you going?" he heard Garrett say.

"To set things right," Tucker replied. He was man enough to admit he'd made a mistake. He just prayed Autumn could find it in her heart to forgive him.

Tucker paused in his front yard, having caught sight of Autumn through the living room window. She was seated on the sofa, book in hand as she read her nightly bedtime story to Blue, who was snuggled up against her aunt's side. Dragging in a deep breath, he gathered up his courage and made his way inside.

Autumn looked up when he entered the room and then stiffened, closing the book she'd been reading to Blue. "That's enough for tonight," she told Blue. "You need to get to bed. We've got a long drive ahead of us tomorrow."

Blue's sleepy eyes lifted. "But I don't wanna leave."

His daughter's words touched his heart. He didn't want her to leave, either. If Autumn would give him a chance to make amends and set things right, maybe things would work out after all.

"I know you don't, sweetie," Autumn replied with a sad smile. "But we've got to get back to Cheyenne."

"Daddy!" Blue said, her tired eyes lighting up the second she saw him standing there in the doorway.

"Hello, sweetheart."

Autumn stood and reached for Blue's hand. "We were just getting ready to go to bed. Come on, sweetie. Give your daddy a good-night hug before we go to bed."

They crossed the room to where he stood waiting. "'Night, Daddy," Blue said, looking up at him with a hint of a pout to her lips.

"'Night, sweetheart," he said, bending to kiss the top of her head. "I'll see you in the morning." If he couldn't convince Autumn to stay, he'd at least be there to see his daughter off until he could get her back through legal means.

As they started past him, Tucker said, "Autumn..."

She paused in the hallway to glance back at him.

"I was hoping you might be able to spare a few minutes to talk after you settle Blue into bed."

"I was under the impression you'd said everything you needed to say already."

A frown tugged at his mouth. "I owe you an apology for the way I reacted earlier."

She studied him for a long moment, as if judging his sincerity. Then her gaze dropped down to his sleepy-eyed daughter. "I'll meet you out on the porch in ten minutes." That said, she led Blue away down the hall.

Less than ten minutes later, Autumn sat waiting for Tucker as he returned from the barn where he'd settled the horses for the night. She was seated on the porch swing, moving back and forth in a slow glide. "That didn't take long," he said.

"Blue was out the second her head hit the pillow."

"May I?" he asked, inclining his head toward the empty space beside her on the swing.

With a sigh, she stopped swinging, allowing him to settle his much larger frame next to hers.

"I'm sorry," he said again as he extended his long legs to set the swing into motion once more.

"No," she said softly. "I'm sorry."

Her apology took him by surprise. "You have nothing to apologize for," he told her, his hand covering hers. "I can't tell you how much I regret comparing your decision to leave tomorrow to Summer's actions," he went on as he settled back against the cool, wooden slats of the porch swing. "You're nothing like your sister. I know that you would never have walked out and taken my daughter away without letting me know of your intention to do so."

"No," she said softly. "I could never have done that to you. No matter what was said between us."

"Speaking of what was said earlier. I talked to my brothers after dinner," he began.

Autumn sighed, nodding knowingly. "When the three of you stepped outside for a spell."

"Yes."

"I reckon they think me an awful person for changing my mind about turning custody of Blue over to you."

He gave a chuckle. "Hardly. My brothers took your side if anything."

Her eyes widened in surprise. "They did?"

"Let's just say they convinced me to put the proverbial shoe on the other foot. And that's when I realized I would've done the same thing if I were in your position. So I asked them if they'd consider buying me out if that's what it took to keep Blue in our lives."

She looked up at him, wide blue eyes reflecting the gentle glow of the porch light. "You would walk away from your part of the business?"

"I told you from the start that I'm willing to do whatever it takes to have my daughter in my life. If selling my share of the business can make that happen, then I'll do it."

Tears sprang to her eyes, a few glistening drops escaping to slide down her cheeks.

"You would do that for Blue?" she said as if his willingness to actually do this was beyond her ability to comprehend. Then again, for Autumn, it might be. Her father hadn't given up anything for his daughters.

"You did," he reminded her with a tender smile. "Selling your real estate business to help support your sister and her little girl—my little girl. Which means you know better than anyone the sacrifices some people are willing to make for those they love."

She nodded, looking off toward the moonlight-shrouded barn. "Yes, I do."

"I want my daughter here with me, Autumn," he said in a gentle plea. "I can't lose her again."

She looked his way. "If you're willing to make that kind of sacrifice for Blue, then you deserve the chance to raise her. It's what Summer wanted."

"But not you," he stated.

"No," she said sadly. "For purely selfish reasons," she added. "But it's Blue's needs that matter most to me. If you're prepared to begin seeing to your daughter's needs, and if it's okay with Blue, she can stay here with you when I go back to Cheyenne tomorrow."

He blinked hard, unsure if he'd heard her right or not. "You'd leave her here?"

"It's not like you're a stranger," she replied. "You're her father."

He was that.

"Look, Tucker, I'd keep Blue with me forever if I

could. But she belongs here. Shuffling her back and forth while custody legalities are being seen to would be too hard on her. I love her enough not to put her through that." She looked up, searching his gaze before adding, "Unless, you'd rather wait."

"No," he said, shaking his head determinedly. "I've waited long enough."

"Yes," she said with a tender smile. "You have." She folded her arms in front of her as if warding off the night's chill.

Slipping his arm around her shoulders, Tucker drew Autumn closer to his side. An act that felt as natural as breathing. He looked down at her, searching her face. "Will you be okay? I know how big a part of your life Blue has been."

She teared up again. "God has a plan for us all. *His* bringing you into Blue's life means He has other plans for me. Maybe returning to the life I once had back in Texas is the path He's guiding me toward."

"Texas?" he repeated. "Why would you think that?"

"Hope called when you were out in the barn, to tell me that she'd heard my real estate business was back up for sale. The woman who bought it from me has decided to retire and move back to Virginia. I think I might put in an offer."

"And leave Blue?" he said in disbelief.

"She won't be with me," she reminded him. "She'll be here with you. And I would visit her often. Just as I used to do before I moved in with her and her momma."

"But Texas is so far away," he complained, his mouth tightening with a frown.

She closed her eyes, her expression pained. "I don't think I can stay in Cheyenne without Blue. Or Summer," she said, her voice catching. "At least in Texas I won't feel quite so alone."

He didn't want her to feel alone. Ever. But the thought of her being more than a thousand miles away... Tucker tried to suppress the unexpected feelings that brought about. He'd never thought he'd ever allow another woman close to his heart, but Autumn hadn't just gotten close, she'd latched on to it. "Don't go."

"What?"

"Stay here," he told her. "Take time to really think this out." He searched her beautiful face, wanting to burn it into his memory as he felt what could have been slipping away. "Do it for Blue. Do it for *us*."

Opening her eyes, Autumn looked up at him with a frown. "I'm not, but taking my time isn't gonna change the way I'll feel when I leave here."

Tucker dragged a hand down his lightly whiskered jaw. "I hate this. I don't want to be the cause of your sadness."

"You're not responsible for this situation we find ourselves in. My sister is," she told him, forcing a soft smile. "And as much as I have loved helping to care for Blue, it never should have been my place to do so. It should have been yours. And now you're gonna have the chance to be the father Blue has always needed in her life."

"I will do right by her," he said, his words tight with emotion.

"I know you will," Autumn said, looking out over the ranch. "She'll be happy here. I know it in my heart."

Tucker found himself wishing for things he had no right to. Because Autumn was Summer's sister. He shouldn't feel anything for her. But he wasn't ready to see her go, not yet. "Are you dead set on leaving tomorrow?"

Worry creased her slender brows. "Are you having second thoughts?"

"Not at all," he replied. "I was just hoping you might consider joining us for the town's annual fall barbecue. It's only a few days away. You'd get to meet more of the people Blue will be growing up around. And, while it's not an actual outdoor barbecue, there is an abundance of picnic dishes to choose from. Did I mention there's an entire table devoted to desserts?"

"An entire table, huh?" she teased.

"Two if that's what it takes to sway you," he said with a grin.

She smiled up at him. "It's working."

If he had his way, desserts wouldn't be the only thing he'd be swaying her over to his way of thinking on. Because the feelings he had developed for Autumn ran too deep for him to just sit back and watch her walk away.

Chapter Ten

Autumn knew that delaying her departure, even a few days, was dangerous to her heart—but she'd agreed to stay anyway. Not that Tucker would ever know how foolish she had been in allowing herself to fall for him. A man she had no right to feel anything for. She'd agreed because she was nowhere near ready to leave Blue, or Tucker for that matter, and her attending the barbecue with them gave her the reason she needed to stay on just a little while longer.

Her gaze shifted to Blue, who was doing pirouettes around the bedroom to make the floral chiffon dress she wore flare out around her. She was so excited to be going to the barbecue and had insisted on dressing up even though the event, according to Tucker, was casual dress.

Her heart pinched as she watched her niece. Tomorrow they would be separated for the first time since Autumn had gone to live with Summer. She and Tucker had sat down with Blue and explained things to her as best they could. Blue had accepted the news that she would be living with her daddy from there on out exceedingly well, which, for Autumn, might have hurt her feelings if not for the fact that her niece had told him that she wanted Autumn to stay, too. *In a perfect world*, Autumn thought with a touch of melancholy.

A horn honked outside. Stopping midspin, Blue ran over to look out the window, waving excitedly at her daddy. Tucker had run into town to help his brothers and several others set up tables and chairs for that evening's festivities.

Autumn crossed the room to the closet to grab their jackets. "Time to go, sweetie. Our carriage has arrived."

"That's not a carriage," her niece countered as she turned from the window and raced for the doorway. "It's Daddy's truck!"

"I take it your daddy isn't really a prince, either?" Autumn called out as Blue disappeared from sight.

She stepped out into the hallway to find Tucker standing just inside the front door, grinning from ear to ear.

"I might not be a prince, but I am charming," he said, that dimple of his deepening. "Or so I've been told."

Autumn laughed softly. "You are that." Looking to Blue, she said, "Here's your coat."

As her niece slipped into hers, Tucker took Autumn's from her hand and helped her into it. "Thank you," she said.

"My pleasure." Opening the door, Tucker made a sweeping motion with his hand. "Your carriage awaits."

Blue gave an exasperated groan. "Daddy, it's not a carriage," she said as she stepped outside. "It's a truck."

"That's too bad," he told her. "Because you look just like a princess this evening. Speaking of which…" he said as he turned back to Autumn.

"I know what you're gonna say," she said, cutting him

off. "But casual dress is not in your daughter's vocabulary when it comes to parties of any kind."

"It's a good thing you chose a career in real estate, because mind reading doesn't appear to be your forte."

She looked up at him questioningly.

Serious green eyes met hers. "I was just going to say that you look really pretty today."

His compliment gave her butterflies. She had chosen to wear jeans and a deep cobalt sweater that brought out the blue in her eyes, and, of course, her favorite pair of high-heeled riding boots. "Thank you."

"You're welcome." Placing an arm at the small of her back, Tucker escorted her and Blue out to his truck.

She wanted to lean into his strength. To keep him by her side forever. But he wasn't hers to keep. Neither was Blue. All she could do was relish the time she had left with him. With them. She glanced down at Blue whose tiny, perfect hand was wrapped snuggly around her own, and wondered how her heart would ever be able to function with her leaving so much of it behind in Bent Creek.

The mouthwatering aroma of barbecued ribs greeted them the moment they pulled up in front of the enclosed park pavilion where that afternoon's festivities were being held. "Mmm..." Autumn groaned. "Will you just smell those ribs."

"Wait until you taste them," Tucker told her as he pulled into an empty parking space.

"I wanna swing!" Blue exclaimed, having spied one of the park's two playgrounds.

"After we say hello and eat," Autumn told her.

They were greeted at the door by Tucker's family

who led them back to the seats they had saved for them. Paper divider plates and plastic silverware lined the tables atop the red-and-white-checked plastic tablecloths. Mason jars filled with baby's breath and white carnations made for very cheery centerpieces. It was so very picnicish that it almost made one forget that winter was just around the corner.

"I hope you brought your appetite," Grady Wade said to Autumn. "There's enough food here to feed the entire county."

Autumn glanced around, finding that Tucker's daddy hadn't been exaggerating. "Starving, actually," she told him with a smile.

"Me, too!" Blue chimed in.

"Why don't we go check out the dessert table," Jackson said in a rather loud, conspiratorial whisper to Blue.

"Honey, she hasn't even eaten yet," his momma scolded, though her words weren't truly reprimanding.

"Desserts are the first to go," he told his momma. "I've learned to grab mine before sitting down to eat or risk getting stuck with something that doesn't quite satisfy my sweet tooth."

"Makes sense to me," Tucker's daddy said.

"Come on, Blue," Garrett said, sweeping her up in his arms. "There's a slice of peach cobbler calling out my name."

"Food can't talk," Autumn heard her niece say as her uncles and grandpa led her away.

"You can't pull anything over on my daughter," Tucker said, sounding like the proud daddy he was.

Tucker's momma stood clicking her tongue. "I'd best go make sure they don't go heaping sweets on Blue's plate like they tend to do on their own. You two go fix yourselves a plate of some real food."

"Don't be fooled," Tucker muttered to Autumn as his momma walked away. "She's going to take her pick of desserts right along with Dad and my brothers."

Autumn muffled a giggle. Then, noting the way Tucker stood watching his family as they hovered around the dessert table, said, "Real food's greatly overrated. Don't you think?"

He looked her way with a grin. "A girl after my own heart." He nodded toward the table of sweets. "Shall we?"

Autumn gave a conspiratorial nod. "Let's."

After being delayed by several people stopping them to exchange idle chatter, Tucker was finally able to work their way across the room to the dessert table.

A familiar voice spoke up from behind them as Tucker and Autumn filled their plates with sweets. "I see you made it."

Tucker turned just as Justin stepped up to join them. "We did," he said with a nod and then looked to Autumn. "You remember my daughter's aunt."

"Not a face many men could easily forget," he replied with a widening grin. He gave a polite incline of his head. "Autumn."

"Justin."

Not a face many men could easily forget? While the compliment was undeniably true, Tucker hoped Autumn could see through Justin's flirtatious words. His friend could be a real smooth talker when it came to females, but he was not the settling-down kind.

"Who knew this town had so many charmers in it?" she said, looking to Tucker with a teasing grin.

Well, he for one didn't care for Justin trying to charm his girl. *His girl?* Talk about getting ahead of himself where Autumn was concerned. But if the night went the way he hoped, that was exactly what she would be. *His* girl. "We were just heading over to the dessert table. Care to join us?"

"Already been there. Got to be quick on the draw to get the best desserts at these things." He glanced around. "I was hoping you'd have brought your little girl."

"We did," Tucker replied. "Blue's at the dessert table as we speak, filling her plate with sweets along with the rest of my family."

Justin looked toward the dessert table, his eyes widening the moment he caught site of Blue. "She looks just like you. Only a whole lot prettier."

"Come on," Tucker said. "I'll introduce you to Blue."

"Let her eat first," Justin replied. "But I'll be expecting introductions before you head home."

He nodded. "You've got it." Looking to Autumn, he said, "Let's go grab ourselves some dessert while there are still choices left to make."

Once everyone had eaten, Tucker turned to Autumn who was seated next to him at the table. "Let's take a walk."

She looked to Blue, no doubt intending to include her in the invite, but his mother jumped in, bless her quick thinking, because she knew what Tucker had in mind. He'd talked to his mom and dad earlier that morning. "You two go on ahead. I told Blue I'd take her over to see Maggie Reynold's new baby. She caught sight of her when we were over at the dessert table."

"If you're sure," Autumn said.

"Go," his mother ordered with a bright smile.

They stood, Tucker placing his hand at Autumn's back as they worked their way outside, their walk somewhat delayed by people wanting to exchange pleasantries.

"I thought we'd never make it out here," Tucker said as they headed for one of several walking paths that ran through the town's park.

"In need of some fresh air?" she teased.

He paused beneath the shade of a large oak and turned to her. "In need of some privacy."

"Privacy?" she said somewhat worriedly. "This sounds serious."

He nodded. "You could say that. I wanted you to know there's been a change of plans about selling my share of the business."

A mixture of hurt and disappointment moved across her pretty face before she looked away. "How am I supposed to tell Blue she won't be staying here with her daddy?"

"Blue will be staying here," he assured her.

"Tucker…"

"Hear me out, Autumn. Please," he said tenderly. "When I went out to my parents' place earlier, my father approached me with an alternative plan. I'll remain in the partnership I have with my brothers, but when rodeo season rolls around my father will accompany Garrett and Jackson instead. I'll stay back and oversee things here with the help of a few part-time ranch hands, just as Dad usually does when my brothers and I are on the road."

"But your momma…"

"Is all for it," he assured her with a smile. "After

going to Jackson Hole, Mom's hooked on camping in their new trailer. Traveling to rodeos would give them that opportunity."

She gave him an apologetic smile. "I thought—"

"You have to learn to trust me," he said with a smile.

Her eyes glistened as she stood looking up at him. "I'm sorry, Tucker. Past hurts sometimes have me expecting the worst when it doesn't exist." She reached out, curling her fingers around his hand and giving it a gentle squeeze. "But deep down I really do trust you, Tucker. And I'm so glad you were able to work things out so you didn't have to give up your share of the business. You deserve to be happy."

He caressed the hand curled around his with his thumb. "You deserve to be happy, too."

Silver-blue eyes searched his own, softening. "I never thought I'd be saying this at the end of my time here, but I'm really gonna miss your cowboy charm, Tucker Wade."

"Not Justin's?" he teased.

"Only yours," she said, her pale blue eyes softening.

"Daddy! Aunt Autumn!"

They both turned to look in the direction from which they'd come.

"Over here!" Autumn replied, slipping her hand from Tucker's.

A second later, Blue came running toward them, his mother doing her best to keep up behind her. His mother gave him an apologetic smile. "The music started. Blue was afraid she wouldn't get to dance with the two of you."

Autumn bent to scoop his daughter up. "Not a chance of that happening."

Before Tucker could protest, before he could tell Autumn that there was so much more he needed to say to her, she was walking away, his daughter curled happily around her.

Chapter Eleven

The next morning, Tucker stood watching as Autumn bent to kiss his sleeping daughter farewell. She turned from the bed, thick tears looming in her beautiful eyes. The sight of which tugged hard at Tucker's heart.

With one last glance back at Blue, Autumn hurried from the room.

He fell in step behind her. "You don't have to leave."

She turned to him as she stepped out onto the porch. "Another day or two isn't gonna make this any easier for Blue or for me."

"What if I want you to stay?"

She looked up at him with a tender smile. "Tucker, you don't have to worry about Blue. She's gonna be happy here. I feel it in my heart. Otherwise, I'd never be leaving without her. And you're gonna be the best daddy ever."

"I wasn't asking you to stay for my daughter's sake."

She searched his face, clearly not understanding.

Unable to piece together the right words, Tucker lowered his mouth to hers hoping to show Autumn without words how he felt about her.

His heart lurched when she leaned into him, hands flattening against his chest as she returned the tender kiss. Any doubts he might have had about her feelings toward him were quickly forgotten.

"Autumn…" he said with a sigh when the kiss ended.

She pulled away with a gasp. "I can't do this. Not again."

"Do what again?" he asked, confused by her words.

"I vowed not to be any man's second choice ever again," she told him, tears in her eyes. "I've already been down that road with a cowboy I thought truly cared about me only to find out I wasn't the sister he would have chosen if he'd been given the choice. I'm sorry, Tucker," she said with a sob. "But I'll never be the woman you want." Turning, she practically ran to her car as Tucker stood watching in stunned silence, his heart sinking.

Autumn couldn't be more wrong. She was the only woman he wanted. The woman he loved. And as she drove away, he knew, without a doubt, that she'd taken his heart with her.

In the three days that followed Autumn's leaving, Tucker tried to stay busy, focusing on his daughter's wants and needs, but Autumn's sweet smile lingered painfully in his every waking thought. Regret like he'd never known before filled him. If only he had told Autumn how he felt sooner. Maybe then they would have had time to work through her reservations.

She'd spoken to Blue on the phone every single evening before his daughter went to bed, but she'd carefully avoided any real conversation with him. He hadn't pushed, wanting to give her time to think things over.

Just as he had done himself after she'd gone. Her parting words had him reexamining his feelings, wondering if Autumn might have been right. That what he felt toward her was somehow related to what he had once felt for his wife. But it hadn't taken him long to put that possibility to rest. While it was true he'd met and married Summer first, that, in no way, made Autumn his second choice.

Any feelings he once had for Summer were nothing more than a distant memory at this point in his life. The feelings he had for Autumn were well beyond the youthful infatuation he once felt for her sister. Their relationship was built on trust and respect and a shared love for his daughter, but there was so much more. He found himself wanting to know everything about Autumn, wanting to comfort her when she was down and laugh with her over even the silliest of things. All those things he could no longer do with her living on the other side of the state, or Texas if the offer she'd talked about making on her old business went through.

"I miss Aunt Autumn," Blue said as she fed Hoss another chunk of apple.

"Me, too, sweetheart," Tucker said with a nod. And he'd wasted enough time letting Autumn think otherwise. Instead of giving her time, which, in hindsight, might have made her think she was right about his feelings for her, he should have done whatever it took to convince her otherwise. She didn't belong in Cheyenne, or even Texas. She belonged here with him and Blue, and it was past time to put that cowboy charm of his to real use and win over Autumn's heart once and for all.

* * *

Would he ever stop filling her thoughts? Autumn wondered with a sigh as images of Tucker's face the moment before he'd kissed her drifted through her mind. So tender. So determined. So Tucker. Oh, how she missed him and his beautiful little baby girl.

The doorbell chimed in the hallway, startling Autumn. She rarely had any visitors out here, and her place was a bit out of the way for salespeople to come calling. Maybe it was someone from work, stopping by to check on her. They knew she had returned to Cheyenne, but had extended her leave another week due to the emotional fallout from having given Blue up. She knew that it had been the right thing to do, but that hadn't made it any easier. Since leaving Bent Creek, she hadn't been able to focus on anything but how much she missed Blue and Tucker.

The doorbell rang again, more persistently this time.

With a sigh, Autumn pushed away from her desk and went to answer it. When she opened the door, a loud gasp left her lips. "Tucker," she said, her hand pressed to her chest in a failed attempt to still her racing heart. Seeing the anxious expression on his face, her gaze immediately went in search of her niece. Then she looked up at Tucker, dread filling her. "Where's Blue?"

"Back in Bent Creek, baking cookies with her grandma," he replied. "Or, at least, she was when I called to let them know I was almost here a few minutes ago."

"Why are you here then if Blue is okay?" Not that she wasn't drinking in the sight of him, noting as she did so that he looked tired. His dark, whiskered chin told her he hadn't shaved for what looked to be days. Was taking care of a child more than he'd been prepared for?

Was that why he was here? To work out some other sort of arrangement?

"I came to tell you that you're wrong."

She blinked hard. "Pardon me?"

"I'm fully aware that you're not Summer, just as you know I'm not whoever the man was who broke your trust. There is only one woman who holds my heart. The beautiful, selfless, loving woman the Lord brought into my life, along with my precious little girl. A woman who's steadfast and responsible. A woman willing to sacrifice her own happiness for a little girl who happens to be very special to her daddy."

Tears in her eyes, Autumn took a moment to let Tucker's heartfelt words sink in. He loved her and only her.

He reached out, laying a hand against her cheek. "I've missed you."

"I've missed you, too," she admitted, leaning into his tender touch.

"My whole life changed the day you came into it," he told her. "Not only did you bring me the most precious gift ever, you gave me a taste of what I'd been living without for so very long—true happiness." His smile widened as he added, "And love."

A soft sob escaped her lips. "Tucker."

"I love you, Autumn Myers," he went on. "And I can't bear the thought of you being as far away as Cheyenne, let alone Texas. Blue and I need you. Come back to Bent Creek and start your own real estate business there. There are office fronts available and I promise to be there for you, doing whatever you need to help you take back the dream you so selflessly gave up to help raise my daughter."

Tears spilled down her cheeks. "I love you, too. And I can't think of anything I'd like more than to be living closer to you and Blue."

"With us if I have my way," he said, sinking down onto one knee.

Autumn's hand flew to her mouth as Tucker pulled a blue satin ring box from his shirt pocket. He raised its lid to reveal a vintage filigree-styled engagement ring perched inside.

"You can set the date," he told her. "I'd never want to rush you into something you're not ready for. But I want you to know that I am in this for the long haul. Say you'll marry me, Autumn. Help me to raise my daughter. Let my family be yours. Share my friends. Even my horses if you have a mind to."

"Oh, Tucker." She felt cherished and loved, and so very wanted. Glancing down at the ring he held so hopefully in his hand, she said with a teary sigh, "It's so beautiful." Everything he'd said had been beautiful.

"I'm glad you like it."

She looked up to see the love reflected in his eyes, and her heart swelled with love for this adorably charming cowboy standing before her, a man willing to risk so much for her. Lifting her tear-filled gaze, she said with a tender smile, "If it's true what they say about *home* being where the heart is, then there is no other place I would rather be than in Bent Creek with the two people who mean the very most to me. So, yes, Tucker Wade, I'll marry you."

A wide grin stretched across his face, putting his whisker-covered dimple on full display. Oh, how she adored that dimple.

"I didn't think I could ever be as happy as I was the day I found out Blue was mine. But I was wrong."

"Oh, Tucker," she said, pressing a hand to her heart.

He eased the antique ring from its nest of blue. "This was my grandma Wade's. I know it's old, and maybe not the style you would have chosen, but I wanted to have something to give you when I asked you to marry me."

"It's perfect," she breathed as he slid the ring onto her extended finger. It was as if the ring had been made just for her. Looking up into his smiling face, she said, "I love it. Even more so because it was your grandma's. And I love you."

"Now about setting that wedding date…" he said with a grin.

Epilogue

"It's time," Emma Wade said quietly as she handed Autumn her bridal bouquet.

"Yay!" Blue exclaimed with a twirl, the knee-length light blue tulle dress she wore lifting as if floating around her.

Autumn didn't have the heart to shush her, despite knowing everyone in the church on the other side of the closed doors had to have heard. This was a day of happiness for so many. Her gaze moved to the ribbon-wrapped bouquet of bluebells and baby's breath she held in her hands. Tucker had special ordered the flowers for their wedding in memory of her sister. It had been such a thoughtful thing for him to do, considering his past with Summer. But then Tucker was that kind of man.

"My sentiments exactly," Tucker's momma said with a smile as she handed Blue the basket of silk rose petals she was to carry with her down the aisle. Ones the same shade as Autumn's bouquet. "Remember what you're supposed to do?"

Her niece nodded. "Put them on the floor so Aunt Autumn's dress can scoop them up."

Emma laughed softly. "Such a smart girl. Now Grandma's going to go take her seat in the pew. When the music starts, Mrs. Pratt will open these doors and then you start down the aisle to your daddy. Your aunt Autumn will be right behind you."

She was so grateful to have Emma there. Tucker's momma had welcomed Autumn into her home for the three months she and Tucker had decided to wait to be married. Tonight, she would be sleeping in her own home, Tucker's home, where they would start their life together raising Blue and any other children the good Lord saw fit to bless them with.

Emma stepped over to give Autumn an affectionate kiss on the cheek. "You look beautiful, honey."

"Thank you, Emma. I feel beautiful today."

"Grady and I are going to miss having you with us, but I'm getting something I've wanted for a very long time," she said with a tender smile. "A daughter."

"And I'm getting something I've only ever dreamed of having. A mother," Autumn said, giving Emma a loving hug.

Tears filled the older woman's eyes as she slipped into the church, closing the door behind her.

Moments later, the organ began to play and the large, ornate church door swung open. And there, at the end of the aisle, stood the man who held her heart, his two brothers by his side.

His gaze locked with hers and a wide smile slid across his tanned face.

Blue gave a quick wave to her daddy, who waved right back, before setting off down the white runner tossing flower petals to and fro with youthful exuberance. As soon as she reached the altar, her niece took her place next to Hope, who had flown from Texas with Logan to be Autumn's matron of honor.

The "Wedding March" began to play and it was all Autumn could do not to run to Tucker in her eagerness to be at his side now and forevermore. Instead, she forced herself to move toward him in slow, mindful steps, taking it all in as she made her way past the rows of friends and family who had come to witness their becoming man and wife in the eyes of God.

As if reading her mind, or perhaps feeling the same need to be by her side, Tucker stepped toward her, meeting her halfway where he crooked his arm. "If it's all right with you, I'd like to start our marriage the way we're going to live our lives together—meeting each other halfway and traveling down the road of life as one."

"I'd love nothing more," she told him as she slipped her arm through his. She would gain so much that day. A husband who loved her, the opportunity to take part in the raising of her precious niece, a family to call her own and a place to finally call home. She was truly blessed.

* * * * *

If you enjoyed this story, pick up these other books by Kat Brookes:

HER TEXAS HERO
HIS HOLIDAY MATCHMAKER
THEIR SECOND CHANCE LOVE

Available now from Love Inspired!

Find more great reads at www.LoveInspired.com

Dear Reader,

Life is filled with choices. Each and every one of those choices we make takes us down a different path. Tucker chose never to marry again after his first marriage failed, living a life he thought was fulfilling enough. It wasn't until the Lord brought Autumn into his life with the daughter Tucker never knew existed that he found himself considering a new path, wanting something more than what he'd settled for. And in doing so, he found true happiness. I believe the Lord provides us with many opportunities to find our own happiness. We just have to be willing to go in a direction that we'd never considered, or, perhaps, were too afraid to.

I hope you've enjoyed sharing Tucker and Autumn's journey. Be sure to look for Garrett's and Jackson's upcoming stories.

Kat

Get 4 FREE REWARDS!

We'll send you 2 FREE Books plus 2 FREE Mystery Gifts.

Counting on the Cowboy
Shannon Taylor Vannatter

Reunited by a Secret Child
Leigh Bale

Love Inspired® books feature contemporary inspirational romances with Christian characters facing the challenges of life and love.

FREE
Value Over
$20

YES! Please send me 2 FREE Love Inspired® Romance novels and my 2 FREE mystery gifts (gifts are worth about $10 retail). After receiving them, if I don't wish to receive any more books, I can return the shipping statement marked "cancel." If I don't cancel, I will receive 6 brand-new novels every month and be billed just $5.24 for the regular-print edition or $5.74 each for the larger-print edition in the U.S., or $5.74 each for the regular-print edition or $6.24 each for the larger-print edition in Canada. That's a savings of at least 13% off the cover price. It's quite a bargain! Shipping and handling is just 50¢ per book in the U.S. and 75¢ per book in Canada*. I understand that accepting the 2 free books and gifts places me under no obligation to buy anything. I can always return a shipment and cancel at any time. The free books and gifts are mine to keep no matter what I decide.

Choose one: ☐ **Love Inspired® Romance Regular-Print** (105/305 IDN GMY4) ☐ **Love Inspired® Romance Larger-Print** (122/322 IDN GMY4)

Name (please print)

Address _____ Apt. #

City _____ State/Province _____ Zip/Postal Code

Mail to the **Reader Service:**
IN U.S.A.: P.O. Box 1341, Buffalo, NY 14240-8531
IN CANADA: P.O. Box 603, Fort Erie, Ontario L2A 5X3

Want to try two free books from another series? Call 1-800-873-8635 or visit www.ReaderService.com.

---

*Terms and prices subject to change without notice. Prices do not include applicable taxes. Sales tax applicable in N.Y. Canadian residents will be charged applicable taxes. Offer not valid in Quebec. This offer is limited to one order per household. Books received may not be as shown. Not valid for current subscribers to Love Inspired Romance books. All orders subject to approval. Credit or debit balances in a customer's account(s) may be offset by any other outstanding balance owed by or to the customer. Please allow 4 to 6 weeks for delivery. Offer available while quantities last.

Your Privacy—The Reader Service is committed to protecting your privacy. Our Privacy Policy is available online at www.ReaderService.com or upon request from the Reader Service. We make a portion of our mailing list available to reputable third parties that offer products we believe may interest you. If you prefer that we not exchange your name with third parties, or if you wish to clarify or modify your communication preferences, please visit us at www.ReaderService.com/consumerschoice or write to us at Reader Service Preference Service, P.O. Box 9062, Buffalo, NY 14240-9062. Include your complete name and address.

LI18

SPECIAL EXCERPT FROM

Love Inspired®

When a former sweetheart reappears in this widow's life, could it mean a second chance at love?

Read on for a sneak preview of
A Widow's Hope,
the first book in the series Indiana Amish Brides.

He knocked, and stood there staring when a young, beautiful woman opened the door. Chestnut-colored hair peeked out from her *kapp*. It matched her warm brown eyes and the sprinkling of freckles on her cheeks.

There was something familiar about her. He nearly smacked himself on the forehead. Of course she looked familiar, though it had been years since he'd seen her.

"Hannah? Hannah Beiler?"

"Hannah King." She quickly scanned him head to toe. She frowned and said, "I'm Hannah King."

"But...isn't this the Beiler home?"

"*Ya.* Wait. Aren't you Jacob? Jacob Schrock?"

He nearly laughed.

"The same, and I'm looking for the Beiler place."

"*Ya,* this is my parents' home, but why are you here?"

"To work." He stared down at the work order as if he could make sense of seeing the first girl he'd ever kissed standing on the doorstep of the place he was supposed to be working.

"I don't understand," he said.

"Neither do I. Who are you looking for?"

"Alton Beiler."

LIEXP0718

"But that's my father. Why—"

At that point Mr. Beiler joined them. "You're at the right house, Jacob. Please, come inside."

He'd never have guessed when he put on his suspenders that morning that he would be seeing Hannah Beiler before the sun was properly up. The same Hannah Beiler he had once kissed behind the playground.

Alton Beiler ushered Jacob into the kitchen.

"Claire, maybe you remember Jacob Schrock. Apparently he took our Hannah on a buggy ride once."

Jacob heard them, but his attention was on the young boy sitting at the table. He sat in a regular kitchen chair, which was slightly higher than the wheelchair parked behind him.

The boy cocked his head to the side, as if trying to puzzle through what he saw of Jacob. Then he said, *"Gudemariye."*

"And to you," Jacob replied.

"Who are you?" he asked.

"I'm Jacob. What's your name?"

"Matthew. This is Mamm, and that's Mammi and Daddi. We're a family now." Matthew grinned.

Hannah glanced at him and blushed.

"It's really nice to meet you, Matthew. I'm going to be working here for a few days."

"Working on what?"

Jacob glanced at Alton, who nodded once. "I'm going to build you a playhouse."

Don't miss
A Widow's Hope *by Vannetta Chapman,*
available August 2018 wherever
Love Inspired® books and ebooks are sold.